A Habit
of
Resistance

FERNANDO TORRES

FIVE TOWERS

PUBLISHING

A HABIT OF RESISTANCE

By Fernando Torres

For all commercial inquiries, please contact:
comments@fivetowerspublishing.com

ISBN-10: 069235901X

ISBN-13: 978-0-692-35901-3

★ First Edition ★

FIVE TOWERS

PUBLISHING

"Do not do it! Why should I be spared? Is it not right that I should gain no advantage from my baptism? If I cannot share the lot of my brothers and sisters, my life, in a certain sense, is destroyed."

Edith Stein, Carmelite Nun

(Discouraging any attempts of rescue prior to her deportation to Auschwitz concentration camp.)

DEDICATION

In memory of all those who opposed totalitarianism during WWII, and for the thousands of nuns, priests, and clergy killed or sent to Nazi concentration camps. Your sacrifices are neither forgotten nor diminished by time.

Table of Contents

PROLOGUE
THE FALL OF PARIS

René's leaden-blue eyes watched the field-grey German troops march from the Arc de Triumph, en-route to the Place de la Concorde. It was an appropriate destination, for all the vermillion atrocities the square had borne. He felt like a specter that others could pass through, as the son of France had reached an emotional state, not unlike what he had known before his nonexistence gave way to birth. Could any of the great Surrealists have imagined the perverse juxtaposition his eyes now attempted to resolve? Paris had become the set piece in a Wagnerian opera whose author, a failed artist, composed fanfiction with the bloody quill of history.

Little did René envision that among their numbers, was one who would cure him of his indifference. He would soon realize that war was not merely a struggle of nations, but a conflict of opposing, individual consciences. Astride a most noble-looking stallion, whose muscles flexed beneath titanium fur, sat a particularly striking looking German. His saber was held to attention and his jaw firmly set. If terror could ever be attractive, then he presented a handsome figure. René had never paused to consider such questions, but then he had never imagined Nazis marching in ranks down the Champs-Èlysées. The music, they played, was upbeat, but his French heart sank with every note.

How had it come to this? Hadn't the Munich Agreement assured "Peace In Our Time?" In March of 1939 the value of giving Hitler the Sudetenland was revealed as Hitler sat down to enjoy the rest of Czechoslovakia, as his complete meal. England and France were so appalled that they rushed to offer their protection to Poland. Hitler, however, had made plans to share his banquet with the Soviets; in exchange for complacency towards its invasion. The Allies had been so willing to accept the loss of Czechoslovakia and Austria, that Hitler felt assured that he could partake in another helping of Europe. Devour it he did.

Poland was no match for the thousands of German Luftwaffe planes that fell from the sky, mechanized dragons of the industrial age. Along the border, they shared with Germany, Polish cavalry brigades were diffused like clearcut patches of oakwood. While, to their credit, they had almost five hundred tanks, it was nothing compared to the two thousand, riveted, bulls that pawed the ground, against them. Panzer divisions of heavy and light infantry charged through the Polish army and ravaged their way to Warsaw. By the first day the Polish Air Force, along with it's airfields, had already been destroyed. The Luftwaffe ripped at the seams of the Polish frontline and draped them in a cloak of despair. The Germans, who had built much of Poland's infrastructure, now bombed it into oblivion, with precision brought on from educated familiarity. Thirty-nine days after the battle's commencement

Poland surrendered. The Poles had suffered nearly a million casualties, while the Germans had lost, but forty thousand.

France, along with England, declared war on Germany; fulfilling their earlier promises to Poland. The French even invaded Germany briefly, but fled upon word of Poland's demise. The fall of Norway had also been inevitable. Without a secure route, for its iron ore, Germany's ability to conduct war would have collapsed. After the Norwegians prophetic defeat Neville Chamberlain, the Prime Minister of Britain, was replaced by his antithesis Winston Churchill. This bulldog of a Brit was a man whose cells bristled with moral resolve and for him, appeasement was a naive fairytale.

Grey sleet fell upon Rotterdam, as Nazi paratroopers attacked the Netherlands, Belgium, and then France. While German divisions pounded the Maginot Line, the main thrust of the attack pierced through Luxemburg and deep into the land of the Gauls. Built at a cost of three billion Francs, the Maginot Line was Christendom's answer to the Great Wall, and it stretched from Switzerland to Luxemburg. With a hundred kilometers of tunnels, its many forts worked in perfect synergy. Yet, it had a weakness. With its impenetrable trees, the Arden forest had been assumed to be Mother Earth's fortress. The French forces there, had not been given sufficient anti-tank or aircraft needed to act. Surely, Germany would repeat its strategy from WWI, it was thought, but that was not to be. One hundred and thirty-six German divisions trampled their borders. Four thousand Luftwaffe planes, twice that of the Allies, harvested their fields.

Why is there always such a beautiful calm before the storm? René wondered. He thought back to those luxurious spring lunches he enjoyed under Parisian horse-chestnut trees. The clatter of easy conversation and clinging coffee mugs, as silver spoons stirred them with sugar and fresh cream. Beautiful young ladies who laughed easily at his pointed observations, their names lost, but their smiles ingrained in his memories. From within eight months of peace, the threat of war seemed barely theoretical. People debated the merits of their situation as if their conclusions could install logic into those who had already succumbed to madness. The clatter that replaced this precious memory was now soldier's boots that aggressively stomped weary cobblestones, and there was nothing abstract about them.

How could such a beautiful, and civilized, way of life prove so fragile? René now understood that Paris and its many pleasures were as fleeting as May's strawberries. The most reasonable choice, was the one that filled him with dread. He would return to Brassac, from whence he had sworn never to return. Brassac with its quaint chateau and stern-looking church, whose nuns had instructed him in what being French meant. Father Jubé, the priest whose title had been a truer characterization of his role in his life, than his robes; would be there wanting. However troublesome though, Brassac was far from Paris and the hopelessness of war. Returning had never been in his plans, but Paris was in chains, and it was painful to observe. Why then did he pause? *How odd*, he thought to himself. He almost feared home as much as the war.

CHAPTER ONE
UNCONVENTIONAL

Sister Marie peered down the u-shaped sight of her 1886 Lebel rifle. Her lips were a touch blue as she held her breath and took aim at the green bottle that saluted from atop a pile of haystacks. The corners of her mouth curled behind the shoulder stock.

"For God's sake, not my Bordeaux! Have you no mercy sister?" Philippe twisted his hat to alleviate his anxiety. "The wife can still use it in the kitchen."

Sister Marie, temporarily, lowered the barrel of her rifle. "Philippe, we have spoken on this matter many a time. You are a drunk."

"I'm French," Philippe protested.

"Then try being half as French," she instructed him. "Your wife needs a husband, not a lush. I enjoy a nice Bordeaux as much as the next nun, but three bottles...in one day--"

Sister Beatrice tsked at him, in exaggerated disapproval.

"But if this is the only way for you to understand...well." Sister Marie raised her rifle and squeezed the trigger. The bottle exploded, and purple mist filled the air with a pungent fragrance.

Philippe made an expression like he was going to cry, but without the adequate hydration to form tears. "Now you've done it. Why couldn't you just use a ruler like when I was a boy?"

"Philippe, I always use the medicine appropriate to the disease." She checked the sight of her gun. "If a ruler would help keep you from coming home intoxicated, then you'd be over my knee this very moment."

A stout-looking French Bulldog approached Philippe and dropped a puppet head at his feet. He looked up, in anticipation of a reaction.

"Robespierre!" cried Sister Dominique, who bore a bit of resemblance to her canine trust. It was something about the way her eyes seemed to calculate weakness. "I don't have time to be putting all the children's toys back together."

Sister Marie snapped the bolt back and reloaded the chamber. She addressed Philippe, in the authoritative tone she saved for such occasions. "No drink for a month and then a glass a day after that. Do we understand each other?"

"Yes, mother superior," he replied, rather chagrined.

"And shave yourself. You look a mess."

Sister Gabrielle, whose low stature made her near-invisible, until she vied for attention, thrust a bouquet of flowers up at him.

"What's this for?" asked Philippe, perplexed.

"Your wife," Gabrielle snapped, surprised at his failure to comprehend the gesture.

Philippe took the flowers and shuffled away with what little dignity he had left.

Sister Marie fired at the target and waited for Sister Anette to retrieve it. "Pretty fine disbursement of shots, but I think I can do better. Sister Anette...be a dear and place the target. Sister Noele, where's the ammo?"

"We haven't any more," she replied, apologetically.

"No ammo? How can we be out already?"

"Well," interjected Anette. "We did knock out the lights at that brothel and remember we shot that wild boar for the Feast of St. Stephen--"

"Did you call Father Jubé?"

From around the corner appeared a handsome looking man, in his mid-forties, trim and clear-eyed. He seemed more the type of gentleman who would frequent Monte Carlo than join the priesthood, but Father Jubé was anything, but predictable. "I noticed a pause in the ruckus, so I figured you might be in need of these," he said and produced a case of 8mm shells. He noticed the splattered wine. "Really? Did you have to shoot a perfectly good bottle of Bordeaux? They're bound to become rare in the months ahead."

"Who says we shot wine?" teased Sister Marie.

"That's grape juice," Sister Beatrice informed him. Older than the others, her trim physique and reading glasses made her look more like a librarian than a nun. Truth be told; she was better read than most librarians. "We emptied the wine into another bottle in the cellarium."

"We figured Phillipe would be too hungover to notice," laughed Sister Noele, the youngest of the group. She had only been a part of the merry gang for a short while, but had already seen her share of mischief.

Father Jubé looked over the nuns who loaded their antique rifles, with military efficiency. "You are a crafty bunch. I should be glad that you are on the Lord's side. Oh, I almost forgot." He removed a formal looking document from his robe. "It's from the Vatican."

"What do they want this time?" wondered Sister Marie.

Father Jubé just smiled. "For you to disband this little gun club of yours. They say it's not in line with your vows or the impression they wish to give of the church."

"I see," replied Sister Marie. "Sister Anette."

"Yes, mother superior?"

"Kindly file this document like the others."

"Yes, mother superior," she replied, dutifully. Anette walked it to where they had placed their targets and pinned it against the haystacks.

The sisters all fired upon it until their opinion on the matter was unmistakable. Sister Dominique used a braided rope to play with Robespierre, who growled with such ferocity he could be mistaken for being mad with rabies. When the nuns stopped firing, the dog ran over to the haystack, grabbed the document and proceeded to make it into confetti.

Father Jubé watched him, with the same expression of concern, and bemusement, that was customary in the village. "I doubt you have much to worry on. Since the Nazis crossed into France, the mail service has been disrupted. This will be the last bit of correspondence we shall see for some time."

"Will we be ruled by the Germans again?" asked Sister Marie.

"We'll soon know. I've heard that an armistice has been signed, but I'm not sure what it means. It seems for now that the fighting has stopped. Much of the government has fled and apparently our mayor along with them."

"The mayor fled? Who then is in charge?"

"God knows, but Brassac is so small, many assume you are."

Sister Marie laughed. "That may be true, but we shall have to do our best to find someone who at least *appears* to be in charge. I'm sure the Germans will do likewise."

Father Jubé never ceased to be amazed of his friend's ability to both lead the hopeless and delegate to the unwilling. The nuns also ran the small school that served the children in their town, and Marie shared many of the responsibilities. "Well, in the meantime, we must do our part to reassure everyone, by going about our lives, as best we can. Yes, I'm sure wine will be essential if we are to endure the years to come."

The first time he saw Marie, she was seventeen. He had a small job delivering loaves of baguette farinée for Monsieur Louvel and as usual, was taking his time with his efforts. Father Jubé or Francis, as he was known in those days, was not nearly as serious as he would later become. Yes, he was most prone to wandering about the nearby villages, weaving perilously close to people on his bicycle, and enjoying the easy diversions of country life. What drew him to the meadow that day, was the musical sound of laughter, though there was bread yet to be delivered, and a fine dinner of coq au vin awaited him at home. His mother braised the chicken with wine made by their uncle, and the family recipe was a closely guarded secret. Francis thought it must be the finest meal in all of France. His opinion remained unchanged, long after his ability to savor it was gone.

One voice rang higher than the others, and he couldn't help, but wonder if it belonged to someone he would like to meet. The air was thick with dandelion seeds, which softened her features the way the starlets appeared in the magazines Monsieur Louvel liked to read. The girls appeared to be playing pétanque, a game where you toss metal balls at a wooden one called a cochonnet. They had made a circle in a gravel field, where they played in teams. There was something very attractive about the joy they took in each other's companionship.

Marie wore a blue and white gingham dress, with short-healed shoes, and her auburn hair was tied up in a matching bow. Francis could not help, but wonder if she was as much a creation of Renoir's imagination as her parents. He ate one of the baguettes that he was supposed to deliver and pretended to take a casual interest in their game. For her part, Marie tried earnestly to win. Having an audience seemed to provide her with additional motivation.

When they had finished, Francis got up to leave, at which point he heard someone yell, "Hé là!"

"Oui?" he replied, surprised to find his presence acknowledged.

"What is your name?" Marie yelled. Her friends stood behind her grinning, in a manner that gave away all her intentions.

He stopped to consider that he might unintentionally identify himself, as the slothful baker's assistant, but the prospect of being introduced to such a beautiful and lively girl was too much to resist. "Francis," he replied. "I'm from Le Bez."

"I know," laughed Marie.

"How do you know?" Francis wondered. He was certain he would have remembered such an unusually confident, and attractive, young lady.

Marie walked straight up to him and grabbed his delivery. "Because my family ordered the bread."

All the girls laughed, hysterically, delighted by Francis' mortification.

Marie leaned close to Francis' ear and whispered, "Don't worry, I'll tell my mother that I ate it."

Francis smiled, not realizing that he had made the most important friend of his life. As the years passed, he drew upon her strength, until he was unrecognizable from the awkward youth who ate her family's bread.

Through the rest of the summer, Marie visited Francis at the bakery under the pretense of needing bread for dinner. It was a bit of a journey, but Brassac did not have a bakery of its own. One day Marie came to look for him, but was told that he no longer worked there.

"I was fired," he gruffly reported.

"What ever for?" she asked.

"Monsieur Louvel said I talked too much to customers." They both laughed, but then Francis became pensive. "I think there might be a war soon, anyway."

Marie became cross and scolded him, "Don't say that. Why would there be war?"

Francis leaned his bicycle against a tree. "Archduke Ferdinand was killed by assassins."

"In France?" asked Marie.

"Not in France...in Sarajevo. I heard it from my father."

Marie laughed. "What does that have to do with us?"

"My dad says Europe is like a deck of cards and if one falls, we all go down."

Marie's brow furrowed. "I don't like to hear you talk like that. We're having too much fun. How can anything bad happen when we are so happy? Now, don't talk about such things and let's go down to the river and look for frogs."

Francis laughed. "Oui. I will not speak about such things, and if you say so...then they shall all have to get along."

"Don't tease me," she snapped and started off on her bike.

"Wait! Wait for me," cried Francis. He was unsure if she was really mad at him, but he would rather not leave on such a maudlin note.

But war, like the plague of old, did come, and Francis was drafted into the French Army. The Armée de Terre, as it was known, had been successful in stopping the Germans east of Paris, but the situation hardly looked hopeful. Marie accompanied him to the train station; his mother too inconsolable to see him off personally.

"Well, please take care of my bicycle," Francis said, plainly.

"Is that all you have to say?" asked Marie. "This may be the last time we see each other. Promise me you'll write. If you don't...I'll hit you so hard when you get back!"

"Okay, I'll write." He knew that she was not, in the least bit, kidding.

"How often?"

"I don't know, as often as I can. I'm going to be busy."

"Doing what?" Marie asked, indignantly.

"Saving France." Honestly, he did not understand how Marie could always fail to see the big picture. Still, Francis worried more about time than bullets. "Promise me something."

"What should I promise?"

"That you won't let the war change you."

Marie thought about his request. "I think we will both change Francis. Even if we survive, we won't be the same people when we next meet. I should have liked for us to go on this way forever."

"Then let us promise to change together," he proposed.

"Will you kiss me?" Marie asked suddenly. "I've never been kissed, and if you don't return--"

Francis laughed. "Don't worry, I'm sure there are plenty of men who would be happy to oblige you."

"But you are the only one I want to kiss," she revealed. "If something should happen to you, I will never know what it's like."

He kissed her immediately, but before she had time to prepare herself. By the time she had recovered, it occurred to her that she had even missed him getting on the train. "Francis, be safe."

"What?" he yelled, out the window.

"Be safe! Be a coward! A coward can still be loved. Dead heroes are only remembered."

"I'll be fine," he laughed. "Don't worry, maybe I will even kiss you again."

Marie blushed, and her cheeks remained red long after the train had departed, and its smoke dispersed into the heavens. She stayed to watch the train disappear until all that was left was a memory from the last moments of her childhood.

It might have been better had they never kissed for like a seed, it created an attachment that grew in the days that followed. News of the horrors of war, from places like Verdun, fueled her imagination. The Battle of the Somme, alone, contributed 200,000 French casualties. She found herself scouring the newspapers for confirmation, of her worst fears, and she pictured herself as a widow of the heart.

Eventually, the first great war came to its morbid conclusion, and Marie returned to the station, where she had said goodbye to the boy who would no doubt return a man. She was more mature and acclimated by years of sacrifice, but compelling in an altogether different way. Francis stepped off the train his smile less boyish, but as familiar as the fields of vines and small country paths they had once had tread together. They embraced, and that is when she noticed his collar.

"I didn't know how to tell you," he replied. "There was need for a chaplain and I decided to apply."

Marie paused to accept this new reality and replied, "No...I'm glad. Most of the men around here died, whether from being gassed or disease in the trenches. I wondered how I could be so fortunate, but now it is clear to me. All that matters is that you're alive and here with me." She hugged him tightly, but now it felt as if she embraced her brother. "Viens avec moi," she said. "Your mom has made you a special meal. Everyone is waiting to see you."

At the small Jubé family cottage, an outpouring of pride and relief had totally consumed them. Marie sat on the porch with Francis and listened, as he explained his decision to become a chaplain and then enter the priesthood.

"I saw things that changed me. There were people who valued life so little-- I resolved not to be counted among them. I can't just think of my happiness...but what I can do for others."

Marie began to cry, both out of pity for herself and as a release of the emotions she had carried since the war began. Francis gave her his handkerchief, but she pushed it aside and ran from him. He was not sure when, or if, he would see her again. As the days passed, his doubts grew still.

For six months, Francis or Father Jubé, as he was now known, worked hard in his new role. It was fulfilling, if not more challenging than he had expected. One day, as he was crossing the twelfth-century bridge known as Pont-Vieux de Brassac, which connects the town over the river Agout, he saw three nuns walking towards him. He nodded and said a friendly, "bonjour," but gave the encounter no further mind. Father Jubé had walked several meters, when he was struck with a startling revelation. He spun around and cried, "Marie?"

The nuns huddled for a moment and then left her to continue, across the bridge alone.

"It's Sister Marie," she corrected, her face a tapestry of trepidation.

He took a moment to consider what it could mean that she had taken to wearing a habit. "Please tell me you didn't do this for me?"

"I want to be near you...even if it is only as brother and sister."

"That is no reason to enter the convent! Becoming a nun is a decision made out of love for others and to God." He was stern and clerical, rather unlike the boy she had known before the Great War. A couple old ladies, not sure how to react to a lovers' spat between a nun and a priest, clutched their flowers and hurried along their way.

"I know," cried Marie. "Don't you think I thought hard about this? I am not so frivolous, as you think. I have made my choice. If I cannot have your love, then the only one worthy of it is God. I will have no other."

Twenty years later, her words still echoed. Sister Marie finished her final shot and looked over at Father Jubé for approval of her technique. She was surprised to see his focus lost in a past that she, herself, often revisited. "Francis, did you see that?"

"See what?" he asked.

Sister Gabrielle handed her the target, riddled with bullet holes.

Marie admired their handiwork and pronounced, "Sisters, I do think we're improving."

Father Jubé picked up several pieces of the letter Robespierre had shredded and concluded, "I'm sure the Vatican would be thrilled."

It seemed that the nuns were always up to some form of roguery, although usually with the best of intentions. Sister Marie's motto was that it was better to ask for forgiveness than bother getting permission. During such times, Father Jubé liked to retreat to his office and pretend that he had no knowledge of whatever trouble was afoot.

His office was well equipped for the duty of a priest although he had yet to figure out how to prevent trouble from infringing upon his sanctum. "How should I know where your automobile is?" he would say, as he'd spot Sister Marie and Sister Dominique pull it back into its spot. "I'm sure it will turn up eventually." He'd wait until the nuns had made their escape before remarking, "Say, isn't that your car parked across the street?"

His prized possession though was what he called, his private library. It contained not only the requisite theology books, but shelves that overflowed with the works of all the great philosophers, scientists, and historians. As trouble brewed across Europe, Father Jubé had added a most uncharacteristic addition. He had hidden the door to his closet behind one of his bookshelves. Already, he had used it to avoid having to answer, for yet, another of the nun's escapades. He looked about to see that no one watched and then moved the bookshelf out of the way. Inside, the room was stocked to the ceiling with food, wine, and ammunition. The nuns were not the only ones in Brassac who were unconventionally prepared.

CHAPTER TWO
THE MAIRE DE BRASSAC

The train counted off rails, which reminded René of running a stick against the pickets of his neighbor's fence, as a boy. His eyes reflected the sunflowers that bloomed by the sides of the tracks, but he could only think that, like France, their beauty would eventually be trampled. Though in his mid-twenties, he slouched like a schoolboy, a form to which he had lamentably regressed. He knew the devil-may-care persona he had so carefully crafted in Paris, drew further away with every bump of the track. In Brassac, everyone knew his foibles and saw him through the pince-nez of his awkward youth. The jaunty attitude, which endeared him in the salons of the St. Germaine; would surely bring condemnation in the sober streets of provincial France.

More than anything he dreaded the conversation he had deferred for the last year. He had convinced himself that he had fled to Paris to embrace new opportunities and to broaden his life's perspective. In the capital, he could learn about the arts and embrace culture. He imagined himself leading discussions at salons and becoming an accomplished writer. Reality found him telling off-color jokes to dancehall ladies, only interested in the next free round of drinks.

He had heard rumors of the aftermath in Brassac, of his

sudden departure, but they were too astonishing to be believed. He had broken a heart, but surely the young lady who owned it, could not have been traumatized to take so rash a course? Truly, he had broken many hearts in Paris, but he was French, and that was practically his cultural imperative. What crushed René, however, was a tragedy whose final act had yet to be determined. The descendants of La Tour, Delacroix, and Rodin were about be ruled by Huns with rockets.

Paris never inquired about his past, nor did it have time for the future. In such a vast and diverse city, you could easily assume someone else would carry the yoke of responsibility. Alas, it was a dream, too beautiful to last. Even during the fall of Paris, the wine yet flowed. Like many, he refused to accept that darkness had fallen over "La Ville Lumière" until he saw the Germans, marching through its streets. Then, as if cold water had been splashed upon his face, he awoke, gathered his effects, and made for Gare de Lyon; and the next train to Brassac.

"Brassac," yelled the conductor. "Le prochain arrêt est Brassac!"

The reality could no longer be denied. While he had forestalled physical danger, now he would have to confront an emotional peril that was terrible enough, to make him reluctant to leave his seat. It was the same train that had spirited him away from the very small station to which he had just arrived.

"Monsieur...Brassac. This is your stop, no?" The conductor eyed, him with equal parts curiosity and concern.

"Oui, merci." René grabbed his leather bag and crept out the train, half expecting to be lynched the moment he set foot in the station. It was quiet, however, and indifferent to his arrival. *This is absurd.* He decided. *I will pretend that I have not a care in the world. If I do not take the situation seriously, how can anyone else?*

His old shop was in the middle of the town square, yet no one bothered him when he appeared and unlocked the door. Surely, they must have thought it curious to see him, suddenly show up, after an absence of eighteen months? It was dusty inside, but not as abandoned as he had expected; nothing that a little bit of cleaning couldn't correct. René's equipment seemed expectant of his eventual return, like a dog who patiently awaited his master's arrival. It was of little use, anyways, as his inventory had all been sold or donated. He sat at his desk and held a piece of wood that seemed to ask if he might carve some purpose and life into it. *If only someone would do the same for me.* He thought.

The bell above his door rang and for a moment, he was transported back to his days as a shopkeeper. Out of instinct, he turned expectant of a customer, but then he dropped the piece of wood which bounced against the planks of his weathered floor.

Sister Noele's lips trembled, and her accusatory eyes welled with tears. Still only a novice, and not yet a nun, she blamed him for the fact that she had yet to be permitted to take her First Vows. Apparently, his return had not gone as unnoticed as he had hoped. The oak planks creaked, as she crossed to where he stood, dumbstruck. She slapped him hard against his cheek, a sound that echoed through his empty shop.

René's eyes moistened, but neither was sure if it was from the sting of her hand or unresolved feelings from their renewed association. He took a moment to absorb the range of emotions that the slap encompassed. "I'm back Noele," he finally said.

Her eyes were embers, but whether from love or hate was indiscernible. She appeared like she might either run into his arms or give him a reason to defend himself. Then, without any further indication of her sentiments, she turned and ran out the door.

René rubbed his face and leaned down to pick up the piece of walnut he had dropped. He returned to his workbench, grabbed a chisel, and began to carve. After awhile, emotionally exhausted, he lay his head on the table and fell fast asleep.

"Wake up René," boomed an authoritative voice. "Wake up!" Seeing that he failed to stir, they grabbed a small dowel rod and struck him with it.

René winced and opened his bleary eyes to find Sister Marie and Sister Noele standing over him. He might have been less troubled to see two members of the Gestapo.

"Sister Noele," Sister Marie commanded, "Tell him what we discussed. Apologize for striking this man."

Still smarting from being awoken by the dowel, he replied, "And what about you, mother superior? That hurt."

"Don't get fresh with me," Sister Marie snapped, and smacked him again. "That's the reason we're here, aren't we? I hit you out of love."

"So did she," observed René. Sister Marie went to strike him again, but this time he caught the rod and politely put it aside.

"I do not love you," corrected Sister Noele.

René smiled and observed, "I have been slapped before," he chuckled, "but never by someone so full of indifference."

Sister Noele stepped towards him and raised the back of her hand.

"Sister Noele, we do not resort to violence to make our feelings known."

René rubbed his head, "That's a relief. I would hate to see what you would consider a true display of force."

Sister Marie picked up the leather, woodworking strop he used to sharpen his tools, and smacked him with it. "Do you want another, René?" She casually tucked a loose strand of hair, beneath her bandeau, then addressed Sister Noele. "You will apologize to Monsieur René...though he is a cad. There are more productive ways to deal with our feelings than with our fists."

Sister Noele began to cry again. "And how should we do that?"

"With our hearts," she replied.

Noele looked at René and cried, "Mine was shattered by the very man you would have me thank for its loss." She ran outside, the bell ringing loudly in the ears of Sister Marie, whose lips were curled with dissatisfaction.

"You will apologize," Marie shouted, as she ran after her; still clutching his strop.

René walked over and fastened the latch. It would seem that he was not safe in Paris or Brassac. Now, quite awake, he decided to clean up his workshop until he heard another rap against his door. Through the window, he again saw the familiar outline of one of the Sisters of Our Lady of Brassac. René winced and scurried to find a place to hide, but she had clearly seen him.

Her eyes rolled back and forth against the small pane of glass within the door. She continued to pound, with great determination until he relented and released the latch. There stood Sister Dominique, obviously put out at having to wait even a moment longer than was necessary. At her side, was her infamous dog, Robespierre, a well-chewed puppet head in his mouth.

René recognized it as one he had made and went to grab it

from him. The dog dropped the head and growled, aggressively until René backed to a more acceptable distance. "Sister Dominique...why?"

"So, you remember me? I didn't think you were in school enough to take notice."

"How can I forget? I still have bruises."

"Well, maybe you should have completed your homework, instead of whittling things in class all the time."

"I made a career of carving things," René protested. "The town is full of my furniture and your school is full of my toys. Apparently...so is your dog."

She flicked his ear. "Don't sass me. I know what you've done. Sister Marie wants to talk to you."

"I am very busy. I can meet her tomorrow, maybe Wednesday of next week?"

Robespierre gave a low growl to indicate his answer was not acceptable.

"Now René. We can do this the easy way...or my way." Sister Dominique had less authority than Sister Marie, but was twice as intimidating. "So that we are clear...I prefer my way." Robespierre snarled, to add emphasis to her words.

"You know, I'm not the little René you knew at the school. I am a man now and--"

"Robespierre, get him," commanded Sister Dominique.

Robespierre latched onto René and began to tear furiously at his pant leg.

"Ok! Fine! Call him off, I'll go," René cried. He was not actually injured, but his pants were torn and the enthusiasm with which the dog worked, made him fear that things might quickly get out of hand.

"Robespierre, heel." The dog immediately stopped and dropped his head to the floor. He whimpered in disappointment at being interrupted in his sport. "Follow me," demanded Sister Dominique. She looked back and saw René still standing in place, a weary eye on her dog.

"Oh, you meant me? I thought you were talking to the dog." René followed them outside and noticed that Robespierre had returned for his chew toy. He followed them around the corner, but was surprised when they did not turn to go towards the church. Instead, they opened the door to the mayor's office, where Sister Marie sat, in all her state, at the desk. Sister Dominique closed the door behind him, and he suddenly felt as if he had been lured into the type of trap used for small animals and scoundrels.

"Sister Noele," said Sister Marie in a commanding tone. "You may proceed."

Sister Noele stepped forward and gave a slight bow, "In submission to my mother superior, and in all humility, I ask for your forgiveness concerning my actions against you today."

René was not quite sure what to say. He had never been at the receiving end of an apology so sincere and contrite. "Well," he replied, "I suppose I had it coming."

"You're darn right you did," agreed Sister Dominique.

Sister Marie gave her a disproving glare. "Thank you, Sister Noele. That will be all."

Sister Noele shuffled out the door, which left the room even more awkward than it had been before; a feat René would not have thought possible.

"Yes, well...it's been nice seeing everyone again. Such a pleasure--" He turned to leave, but Sister Dominique blocked the door.

"Oh, we're not done with you yet," replied Sister Marie. "Please have a seat." She waited for René to take his place, and her memories retreated to the times when his behavior had challenged the order of the school. He would always be eleven to her. "So...how are things in Paris?"

René was not sure that he wanted to engage in small talk. He knew that Sister Marie was merely preparing him for her real purpose, and he would not know peace until her will was determined. He rather wished she would simply get to the point, but that was not the way things were done in Brassac. "The cafes are full with customers and in the parks and playgrounds, the children still laugh. The fall of France is like a disease that occurs

24

in fits and starts. The patient only knows how bad their situation is when the pain is severe."

"Now that you are back, will you reopen your shop?" Sister Marie asked. She sipped from a cup; her pinkie finger extended.

"No, I think not. I sold all my inventory, and it would be difficult to restore it during such times. I have been carving things out of habit."

"But you loved what you did? You made such beautiful toys, and the children so adored them. I saw a table you made, on a visit to one of our parishioner's estates, and it was very elegant."

"I don't think there is any use for playthings during such times, and the roads are full of discarded furniture." It was the very argument he had already convinced himself with, on the train from Paris. "I will probably have to find a new trade."

Sister Marie did not disagree. "Tous en faverur."

"Oui," replied Sister Dominique. Robespierre snorted.

"Congratulations then...you are the new maire de Brassac."

René looked at her perplexed. "I'm sorry. What is that you just said?"

"You are the new mayor. I am far too busy to continue in the role, and you are in need of a supplementary career. The only condition is that you supply the children of Brassac with as many toys as you can manage. Father Jubé also needs a new chair."

"That is all well and good, but I wouldn't know how to be a

mayor," he protested. René was not sure that he wanted to embark on a political career, but he also knew he did not want to collect firewood for extra income.

"René...we will all have to do things, in the years ahead that we have no desire to do. Do this as an act of atonement for all the people who were affected by your sabbatical in Paris. If you are to remain in Brassac, you will have to contribute. Your choice is whether or not you wish to stay."

René looked around the office and thought that it suited him quite well. Sister Marie rose so that he could try on the chair, and he even began to raise his feet until the sight of Sister Dominique's disapproving glare, caused him to place them back on the floor. "Ok, I will do it. How much trouble can one little town be?" He noticed an opened envelope that he assumed the former resident of his newly acquired position, had abandoned. Inside, were his instructions as an official member of the newly formed Vichy government. René was not as astute in politics as the former office holder and was not really sure what to make of the document. All, he understood, was that as long as order was maintained, the Germans would stay in the occupied territories. Little did he know that it would soon become difficult to tell where Vichy, France ended, and Nazi Germany began.

Sister Marie left René to mull over his newfound responsibilities. She felt positively buoyant, as she walked along the cobblestone path back to the church. Maybe it was unfair to saddle René with such affairs, but it was her way of providing him absolution for how he had treated Sister Noele; while serving the needs of the community in general. She had enough on her plate, with the needs of the school and overseeing France's quirkiest gaggle of nuns.

Appearing around the corner, on his bicycle, was Father Jubé. He wore a smile that always reverted her to nineteen, again. She knew she was not supposed to feel romantic love, but it took all the discipline she could muster to channel her emotions into platonic admiration.

"Did he take the position?" he inquired, with a grin. His respect for her made it more of a rhetorical question.

Sister Marie took a second to collect herself. The sight of him on his bicycle forced too many memories, but fortunately he was not carrying any bread. "Yes, he will do it."

"Did you give him a choice?" he laughed. She had proposed the idea to him, shortly after their mayor had fled; and before René had even returned.

Her eyes were mischievous and full of an energy that, also, caused him to see her outside of their present context. "Of course not. René has always required a push in the right direction and pushing is my spécialité. They both laughed. "He's a good boy--"

"Man," corrected Father Jubé. "He's no longer the child I had to put over my knee when he took apples from the church orchard."

She could see that Father Jubé was teasing her, but she did not mind in the least. "Oh, I suppose you're right. I always act first and think about the entanglements later."

"That is your finest quality." Now it was obvious that he was having fun at her expense, but then he was the one who, often, covered for her various adventures into the gray regions of morality. "Others wonder what they should do, but you act. That is why you are a leader. This town needs somebody who is not afraid of what will happen if they make a choice."

Sister Marie helped him steady his bike by gripping its handlebars. She looked up and wondered if she was, inappropriately, close. "I wish I could be more like you, Francis. You consider all the consequences and when you finally act it is the direction we should have gone, all along. I usually have to double-back, or ask for help."

"Knowing you need others is a true sign of strength. René will need our support and advice, since our government has decided upon the path of collaboration with the Germans."

Sister Marie had heard about Philippe Petain's meeting with Hitler and felt ashamed to have passed her, admittedly, temporary responsibilities to René at such a time. She wondered if she had done so because she was aware that the worst was yet to come.

"How do such things happen? No one I know agreed to such a thing?"

"Benefit is the only blindfold required to convince ourselves that poison is wine. Liberty's comfort level rises and falls with the sympathies of its children. Well, I for one will not collaborate."

Sister Marie looked at the sole man she had ever loved and knew that she could never have possessed him. He was above romantic entanglements. The closest she could ever be to his world, was the path she had chosen. It was enough to work by his side and share his triumphs and sorrows. Her only desire was to grow old beside him, but now his words made her afraid. "I will not let anyone hurt you," she revealed. She knew, immediately she should not have let the words escape her lips, and yet she repeated the sentiment. "I could not bear it."

CHAPTER THREE
THE ROAD FROM INDIFFERENCE

Sister Marie craned her neck to peer around Sister Noele's veil. "Sister, are you wearing makeup?"

"No, mother superior. My cheeks are just flush from the weather. I must be a bit cold--" Caught unexpected, Noele was a doe caught in her hunter's crosshairs.

Sister Gabrielle's eyes rose, inquisitively, over her book.

"Well, mine aren't flush." Sister Beatrice slung her rifle over her shoulder.

"Yours haven't been flush since 1923," replied Sister Marie. "Are you running a fever?"

"I hope it's not contagious!" Sister Anette cried. "Maybe we should put some onions in her socks?"

Sister Noele retreated to a corner and pretended to read. "I'm fine. Really, I'm just cold."

"Then be sure to take a jacket," Sister Marie offered. "We can't have you getting sick with Easter a few weeks away." She put a case of shells in a pouch she had received as a gift for her birthday. Sister Anette had embroidered the likeness of Saint Hubert, the patron saint of hunters, upon it.

"She's not sick," interrupted Sister Gabrielle. "She's in *love*."

There was a clamor as someone dropped their bullets, and they pattered upon the floor. Robespierre sensed something was amiss and barked.

"That's not true!" cried Sister Noele. "I'm fine. Someone make that dog be quiet. He's giving me a headache."

"Robespierre, tais-toi!" commanded Sister Dominique. "It's because René's come back. That's what it is!"

Sister Noele flung herself on the bed, in a way that did not dispel their suspicions. The soles of her shoes offered her silent retort.

"Everyone just leave her alone," directed Sister Marie. "Naturally, René returning to town would make things difficult for her, but we all have feelings. We're not a gaggle of gargoyles, regardless what people think. We're women."

"I'm not a gargoyle!" Sister Gabrielle proclaimed.

"Sorry, sister." Sister Beatrice and Sister Anette agreed while Sister Dominique readied her things and pretended to not be aware that it was her turn to reciprocate.

"Well, I suppose those quail aren't going to just jump on our dinner plates," Marie laughed, knowing that she was not going to be able to pull anything resembling empathy from Dominique. "Sister Noele, why don't you stay this time and help get things ready for when we return with our catch? That would be such a great help."

Seeing the nuns, with rifles slung over their shoulders, was something the town was used to. Not an eyebrow was raised save one gentleman who stopped to remark, "Say something is not right here...where's Sister Noele?"

"She's taken ill," Sister Marie replied.

"Lovesick," croaked Sister Gabrielle.

The gentleman was slightly hard of hearing. "What's that?"

"We were just going to do a little hunting," Sister Marie shouted. "Some nourishment, to help our ailing sister."

"Well, good luck," he offered. "I saw some quail near the Mouyal family's farm."

"Beaucoup obligé," she replied, with a smile.

"So what should we make with them?" asked Sister Beatrice.

Sister Anette shook her head, disapprovingly. "Oh no sister. Never count your blessings before they happen."

"If I were as bad a shot as you, I'd be making plans to eat salad," Sister Gabrielle laughed.

Sister Dominique took up where her epigrammatic sister left off, "I can practically shoot them from here. Why...those quail are as good as stew. We'll roast and serve them with root vegetables--" She lifted her rifle to demonstrate her bladed-off stance. Her attention shifted, however, to a man who appeared to be shaking a child, quite aggressively. "Sister Marie, what's that? What does that awful man think he's doing?"

"Who is he? Do you know him? Maybe it's a family dispute?

I don't, at all, like the way he's handling that child!" She began to run in the direction of the conflict, and the nuns followed her pace. Sister Marie was never shy of involving herself in other people's affairs. Some might think that avoiding the passing of judgment was a virtue, but she saw it as a shirking of responsibility.

When they had gotten within shouting distance of the dispute, the child recognized them and cried out, "Sister Marie!"

"Jacob? Is that you child?" She grabbed the man and pushed him back. "What exactly do you think you're doing?"

The man appeared rather shocked at her involvement. "Madame, he was putting up this poster." Upon it was a picture of Mussolini and written, "L'ami de Monsieur Pierre Laval..." or "The friend of Mr. Pierre Laval." He looked at her as if he awaited an apology.

"Are you trying to say the current government is not friends with Mussolini or Hitler for that matter?" Sister Marie was not interested in getting into a political discussion. She only desired to help the young boy who, although not one of her students, sometimes appeared to play with the other kids.

"He is trying to make the government a fool."

"Oh, the government does quite fine on its own," Sister Beatrice proposed.

"It is propaganda," protested the officer. "He will have to

come with me."

"Now, please...he's a local boy. Let me take him to his father. I will see he gets whatever punishment is appropriate." Sister Marie took the boy's hand, but the officer grabbed the child's shoulder, which put a stop to her.

"He is going nowhere, but with me. This is propaganda dropped by the RAF. He is a traitor, and if the Third Republic taught us anything, it is the perils of being soft." The man grabbed the leaflet back from Sister Marie, all the while trying to break the boy free of her grip.

"He has strong opinions, which is only natural...he's French."

"That is debatable, he is coming with me," and the man drew a revolver, which he addressed at Sister Marie.

The other nuns looked at each other, in disbelief. Pointing a firearm at a member of the cloth was incomprehensible. Sister Anette turned to Sister Beatrice, who was usually the one to bring logic to unfathomable circumstances.

"Now, put that down," Sister Beatrice demanded. "Can't you see this woman is a nun? You don't really think you're going to shoot her do you?"

"I will do whatever I have to," the officer replied. "This boy is an enemy of France and if she will not step aside...so is she."

"I'm not going to let go, so you'd better prepare to shoot me," Sister Marie challenged him. "Neither of us are enemies of France and if this is what the new government stands for; then you'll get no apologies from me."

"Oui," agreed Sister Beatrice. "If Vichy is for such things, then it is not of France. Please leave us, monsieur."

"I am most serious. I will fire," the Vichy officer, reiterated. He said it in a plainspoken manner that sought to relieve them of any doubts.

"Not if I pull first," Sister Dominique revealed, having placed the barrel of her rifle against his back. Robespierre growled, supportively.

The man looked out of the corner of his eye and saw the outline of Sister Dominique, "Oh, what a shame. Now I shall have to arrest you, as well."

"I don't think so," Sister Gabrielle concluded and raised her rifle. "Let them go."

He looked down, at the diminutive looking nun, and began to laugh. "I don't think you understand your predicament. I fought in the First World War. I was a soldier....a trained killer. I do not care that she is a nun; I'm not even religious. I *will* shoot her. I'm surprised you even have the courage to hunt quail. You will not fire, even if I pull this trigger."

"I'll go," said Jacob, suddenly. "Just let the sisters go free. I know I shouldn't have done it. Please--"

The officer tsked, "You're admission of guilt is touching, but I can't just let these women go free after they addressed their rifles at me. They are traitors of the state, and they won't be the first clergy to see bars. Yes...anyone, who is opposed to the new order, is arrested. Especially, your type."

"And we cannot let you take this boy to a camp from which he won't return," replied Sister Dominique.

The Vichy officer pierced his lips, and his eyes squinted, in acknowledgment of the strength of her logic.

"So how are we going to end this?" Sister Marie wondered. "You insist on taking us all to jail and we have Easter services approaching."

He nodded his head, as if he sympathized with their predicament. "Yes, I think you are right. I shall have to end it. We can't stand here all day, after all." He cocked the trigger of his gun. There was a loud bang and then a faint smell of nitroglycerine. The officer looked at his chest and was surprised to discover that blood seeped from his shirt. The gun slipped out of his fingers, and he just crumpled to the ground.

Sister Dominique's rifle lowered, but she did not bother to chamber the next round. Instead, she moved in slow motion, as she processed the result of her decision. Robespierre looked up, expectantly, awaiting his next instruction.

"We have to help him," Sister Marie commanded.

Sister Beatrice attempted to stop the flow of blood, but her efforts proved futile. "He is beyond our help. This man is dead."

"What are we going to do," cried Sister Anette. "What if someone heard?"

They dragged the body behind some hedges.

"Let me take care of him," offered Jacob. "I have a shovel at my house. If we all stand here, someone will see--"

"He's right," agreed Sister Marie. "We need to leave at once."

Sister Gabrielle noticed that Sister Dominique had hardly moved from the spot where she fired her gun. "He was about to shoot Sister Marie. The only reason, you shot him first, was because I was too slow."

The nuns shuffled back to Brassac, but not in their usual manner. There was no laughter, or banter, as they trudged back to the convent. Convent is a bit of an overstatement for what was merely a small collection of rooms next to the church. Decorated with religious icons, and artwork given to them by their students, it was their sanctuary from the moral tempest they could never, truly, escape. They quietly put away their rifles, not yet ready to give voice to their conflicted thoughts. Sister Dominique cleaned her rifle, while the others gave her the room, to process what had happened.

Father Jubé entered all smiles. "So how many quail did we catch?"

"None Father," replied Sister Anette.

"None?" stammered Father Jubé. "How is that possible? You must not have seen any? It is often said that the nuns of Brassac could hit a pheasant in England."

"Bad luck I'm afraid," covered Sister Marie. "I guess we can make a salad with what we have in the garden."

"Truly, these are dark time," Father Jubé laughed.

"You have no idea," Sister Dominique agreed. She finished re-assembling her rifle and placed it back in the cabinet.

Sister Marie put her hand behind Father Jubé's back and proceeded to walk him to the door. "We'll call you when dinner is ready. We just need a few minutes to get everything in order."

In thru the door came Jacob, his face covered in dirt. "I buried him," he cried.

"Buried who?" asked Father Jubé.

"His dog," replied Sister Marie. "He just couldn't let him go."

Father Jubé sighed, "My son...I know it is hard, but you must let him go. It is not sanitary." He looked at Sister Marie and smiled, "We must all learn to let go of things we love. Some things we never truly get over, but still we must let them go."

Sister Marie rolled her eyes and gestured for him to play along.

"Oh, yes, I understand," replied Jacob. "Thank you. He was such a good dog, but I will never forget him."

Sister Beatrice pushed them both out the door. "Thanks both of you, but now we have important business to attend to. Jacob, tell your father hello for us." She slammed the door and latched it fast.

Sister Noele, who had watched from the hallway, sensed something was wrong. "What on earth is going on? Are you all in trouble...again?"

"Far beyond the usual," replied Sister Anette.

"Now Sisters, we must carefully weigh what has transpired." Sister Marie uncrossed her arms, to reveal blood on her white coif.

Sister Noele stumbled back onto one of their stools.

Beatrice removed Marie's coif and began to wash it. "Mother, should I use lemon juice?"

"I should think some salt might help," Sister Anette offered.

"Why is there blood?" cried Sister Noele. "Something tells me that isn't from quail."

Sister Marie sat beside her. "No Sister Noele, that is not from a quail."

"Are you hurt?"

"No, I'm fine. It's not my blood." Sister Marie found a towel and wiped her face.

Sister Noele looked around the room and took stock of her sisters. "Then whose blood is it?"

"Oh, he's not with us anymore," replied Sister Dominique, as she tossed Robespierre a biscuit. "Don't give it a thought, child. Not even a thought."

"Well, we shall have to give it some thought." Marie gathered everyone close. "To answer your question," she revealed, "a Vichy officer was about to shoot me and Sister Dominique...well, she ensured that he was not able to."

Sister Noele stepped back mortified at Sister Dominique, who seemed more occupied with her dog than the moral consequences of the matter. "You shot him?"

"Only once," she protested.

"Is he okay?" asked Noele.

"It's doubtful he'll recover," conceded Sister Dominique.

"Yes, especially now that Jacob has buried him," Sister Anette added.

Sister Marie shot her a look as if to indicate that she was not helping the conversation. "Sisters, I cannot expel a member for something that, given the opportunity; I would gladly have done myself. If I am consumed with any reservations, it is at having put everyone in such a position. If only I had fired...all the weight of this would be upon me instead."

Sister Beatrice placed her arm around her shoulder, "No, mother. Then it would be you who was troubled. If there is any justification, it is that violence was about to be committed, so it only made sense that it was not upon innocents."

"I see what you mean," Sister Marie reflected, "and that is the crux upon which this moral dilemma rests. If even the most open hand is forced into a fist, how terrible is war!"

"What shall we do now?" Sister Noele wondered.

"Why...we shall have to eat salad, of course," replied Sister Anette. "We were not able to hunt a single quail."

It seemed to Sister Marie that there were issues yet to consider. She wondered if talk of dinner was simply the other sister's way of redirecting the conversation back to the banality of everyday discourse. "However, if we were morally obligated in this circumstance, then in what other areas might be not be doing our utmost?"

"What are you trying to suggest?" asked Sister Noele.

"If the Vichy government is evil, don't we have an obligation to do something about it?"

"We are nuns," explained Sister Beatrice. "We serve our community. That is what we do."

Sister Marie was not yet ready to let the issue rest. "Yes, that is what we have always done, but if these are extraordinary times, our regular service might not be enough. Isn't the essence of service being willing to go beyond one's area of comfort?"

"I am not comfortable with where this is going," objected Noele. "Now what should I prepare for dressing? A vinaigrette perhaps? Do we have any les échalotes?"

"Yes, you're right. Let's not talk about Vichy or Germany. You know, the lilies are blooming, and they should be so beautiful next week." Sister Marie put her clean coif on and smiled as if nothing had changed. It was a denial of the actuality of their present circumstances. Nothing would ever be the same. She could not reset the order of things, any more than she could end the war. Change had come, and all the responsibilities it entailed.

CHAPTER FOUR
ENTER THE PUPPETEER

Klaus looked out from his black Škoda Kfz. 21 cabriolet. It was an acceptable staff car, but what he longed for was the Daimler-Benz G4, favored by the who's who of German officers. There was little chance he would be able to acquire such a vehicle, however. He had already concluded that his, so called, "promotion" was nothing more than an attempt to send him as far away as possible. The fact that he found himself, head of the Gestapo, in such a provincial and backwards part of France was proof enough that many of his superiors had found his performance in Poland lacking. He looked at Brassac and let out a small laugh that dripped with condescension. "It reminds me of a Monet painting, but absent the charm."

His lieutenant and right-hand man Friedrich was an abbreviated, vicious man who spoke from his nostrils. The effect was not unlike a congested snarl that made most people, who encountered him, quite uncomfortable. Friedrich observed people's shadows as they attempted to scurry ahead of his gaze and replied, "Half my family died in the Great War, and I'm delighted to see them put under the boot."

"Friedrich, you really missed your calling."

"I did?" Friedrich could not imagine a better post than under

Klaus Metzger, the finest Hauptsturmfürer the German Reich had ever produced, or that is how he saw it. Few within the SS shared his opinion of his master.

"You could most definitely have been a poet." Klaus looked around for a sign that might indicate the office he sought, "If you did not have such a Germanic soul, you could have written sonnets." Friedrich looked at him both perplexed and full of admiration; a common expression in regards to his master. "Friedrich, I really don't want to have to talk with any of these people. Could you please hop down and see where the mayor might be found?" He continued to talk to himself as he adjusted his gloves, "He's probably nearby...no doubt feeding his pigs."

Friedrich jumped out of the car and proceeded to jab at people, who seemed baffled by his strong Franconian accent. Finally, someone was able to determine what he was trying to say and pointed him in the direction of René's office.

The whole situation was really more than Klaus could bear, but if the collaborationist militia were not so incompetent, he might not have been sent to oversee them. Perhaps if he had not been so opinionated in his views on policy matters, and those that had created them, he might have been stationed in Paris. Klaus had determined to use more finesse than he had in Poland, but with more persuasion than the French collaborationists.

Klaus stepped into René's office and found him behind his

desk putting together a wooden airplane model. "Am I in the mayor's office?" There were carpentry and woodworking tools, strewn about; that René had brought over from his workshop.

René glanced up and was alarmed to see an imposing-looking Nazi official. He was, probably, in his late-thirties and dressed in a black SS uniform; whose purpose seemed to be to intimidate him. It was, apparently, having the desired effect. "I am the mayor," René stammered as he tried to hide the toy within his desk. "Please, won't you come in?" He did not recognize him from their chance encounter, shortly after the fall of Paris.

Klaus removed one of his gloves and entered, without any acknowledgement that permission had been granted. "I am Klaus Metzger; the senior Gestapo officer assigned to the Tarn department. I have been assigned to work with the local Gestapo, militia and regional leaders, such as yourself, to address any resistance and ensure that this remains the bucolic place that it was before the war." He strolled around René's office and pitied its rustic, provincial furnishings.

"A goal I can assure you all of us share." René smiled and poured himself a drink to steady his nerves, but neglected to offer his German counterpart the same courtesy. Not a day had passed, since France had fallen, that René had not gazed out his window and wondered when such a man would arrive. The meeting had always been inevitable, but now he found that the overall

45

anticipation had frayed his nerves.

"There have been resistance activities nearby and my dossier contains the notation that a police officer has disappeared." Klaus had returned to his usual curt approach.

"That was some time ago," observed René. "We believe that he probably defected. I'd completely forgotten about it."

"Well, we have not," scolded Klaus. "There have been other incidents that suggest this is not quite the idyllic country paradise." Klaus looked at a puppet that René had hung nearby. He lifted a string and watched one of its hands animate. "Perhaps you have not done all you could to cooperate with such investigations?"

René did not like the insinuation that framed the German's line of questioning. "Of course, I have done everything, but we are not equipped for such large scale investigations. The last thing, anyone in Brassac wants, is trouble. We are very far from the war, and we like to keep it that way."

Klaus let out a sigh. He did not like being reminded that he was so distant from the action that might validate his abilities. "And now I am here to ensure that any trouble is dealt with and...oh yes, I can be quite helpful in such matters. Snuffing out troublemakers is my speciality."

"That is so nice to hear," replied René is a way that was not at all convincing. "Do you enjoy wine?"

"Do you think because I am German, I do not enjoy wine? Do

you not know of Riesling and Sekt? You French are so proud."

René tried to reassure him, but his efforts were not as political as he had hoped. "I enjoy German wine, even though it is a bit acidic for my taste."

Klaus stomped the floor with one of his knee-high boots. "I will not have the mayor of a French town disparage German wine. We will go and drink now!"

"Um, I was actually about to--"

"I have some Spätburgunder that you will try, and you will then see how good German wine is!" Klaus put on his leather gloves and headed for the door.

René sighed and realized that he had no choice, but to join Klaus for a drink to which his opinion had already been decided.

"What on earth is that?" asked Sister Anette.

Sister Dominique looked it over with a critical eye. "It's a Tiger. A German tank."

"Why is it here?" asked Sister Noele. In her day-to-day interactions, there was not much time to consider that France was under foreign influence. Something about seeing the tank, with its Germanic markings, rather underlined their situation.

Sister Marie beat upon it, to test its solidity. "The zone libre is occupied now. Don't you read the newspaper? The Germans are no longer leaving us to ourselves. No matter, unoccupied France was always a lie anyway."

They examined the tank's impressive hull armour with its 88 mm gun. Such a brutish instrument of war was never before seen in Brassac, let alone with its barrel addressed directly at their church.

"Well, I don't like it here," remarked Sister Noele. "It scares me. What if it went off and destroyed the sanctuary?"

"Neither do I," concluded Sister Marie, as she climbed up to its turret. "I think I shall ask them to leave."

Sister Anette watched, befuddled. "Oh? Will that work? Mother superior--"

"They can park this outside of town," Marie replied. Unlocked, she was able to, simply, lift the hatch. "I don't see anyone. I'd better take a look inside."

The sisters watched her disappear and began to panic. Sister Noele cried out, "Please mother! You're going to get in trouble. Someone's bound to come back!"

There was a growl as the tank's V-12 Maybach engine surged to life. Sister Anette jumped out of the way, and the tank lurched forward. The other nuns watched, helplessly, as its treads gripped the cobblestones, and it moved down the road with great speed. Soon it had vanished, entirely, leaving them afraid for Sister Marie, but not sure how to give her aid.

Two tank pilots emerged with cigarettes and several bottles of wine, to find that the object of their trust had disappeared. A cigarette fell from one of the pilot's mouth. He yelled something in German, to which Sister Dominique responded by pointing in the opposite direction. It must have resonated with them for they took off, at once, running in that unfortunate direction.

"What do we do now?" asked Sister Noele.

"She'll be back," replied Sister Beatrice. "Let's go home and pretend like nothing has happened. We have enough of a reputation that someone is bound to come to our door looking for answers."

An hour went by, with nary a sound. The nuns shared their paranoia, as they tried to occupy themselves.

"Have you finished the lesson for tomorrow?" Sister Anette wondered aloud. "The children are studying transitive and intransitive verbs."

Sister Noele looked out the window, "Someone's coming. What do we do?"

"Look natural and don't forget to smile when you welcome them." Sister Dominique seemed to have life experience that went beyond her current responsibilities. Her family had been involved in businesses that crossed the lines of both legal and social norms.

"Is it Marie?" asked Sister Anette.

"No," Noele replied, despondent.

Knock. Knock.

"Ready everyone? Answer it," instructed Sister Dominique.

Sister Beatrice unlatched the iron lock, and the wooden door creaked open to reveal their mayor.

"Monsieur René," cried Sister Noele, relieved. "Or do I call you mayor?"

"René is fine," he said, with a modest smile. He took his hat off and sat on a wooden stool in their eating area. "You know, I helped make these stools...when I was a boy. Father Jubé was teaching us crafts. Maybe, that gave me my career?"

"I remember," replied Sister Beatrice. "He was so young and enthusiastic in those days. He seldom comes to the classroom anymore."

"Well, he's a busy man," René observed, quick to defend his former teacher. "He has many masters to respond to...as do I." He palmed his hat and elevated its brim. "One of mine just came to see me, and he was very upset about a certain tank that had gone missing."

The nuns looked at each other, unsure how they should respond.

"Is this like a toy tank or an actual one?" Sister Anette had a manner of lying that was more comical than convincing.

"Don't be so coy," René protested. "A group of nuns were seen in the area shortly before it disappeared."

"Well, as you can see," snapped Sister Dominique. "We haven't got any tanks. If you want a rosary, then you've come to the right place."

René nodded, as if he was thinking, *So that is how it is going to be?* "So tell me...where is Sister Marie? I see everyone here is engaged in various tasks, but I do not see the ringleader."

"She's busy," replied Sister Anette. "Maybe she's in the sanctuary?"

The mayor let out a small laugh, "Naturally, that is the first place I checked. I also looked all over town, and it is such a small place. Do you not know that I am on your side, but if I do not understand the facts, how can I be of help? So let me ask again, where is Sister Marie?"

"René, did I not teach you better than to show so little respect?" Sister Marie appeared at the back doorway in nothing, but a towel. Her hair dripped with water, and she looked quite perturbed. The mayor was so shocked, at seeing her in such a natural state, that he toppled the stool and broke one of its legs.

"Mother superior, I had no idea..." he stammered.

"That I took baths?" she laughed. "Yes, I too get dirty when I work in the garden.

René covered his eyes, with his hat, and collected the pieces of the broken stool. "I'll fix this for you. Sorry. Sorry for any trouble." He backed out of the room and exited, without permitting himself to look in Sister Marie's direction.

The nuns watched from the window as he scurried down the road before they allowed themselves to laugh, both at his reaction and out of relief at seeing Sister Marie unharmed.

"Holy Moses, where have you been?" asked Sister Beatrice.

"At the bottom of the lake with the tank," she replied. "Why do you think I'm drenched?"

"Oh, we should all go and take a swim sometime!" Sister Anette proposed. "Wouldn't that be lovely?"

Sister Marie just ignored her, but lowered her towel to reveal a large scratch. "I had a little trouble getting out of the turret, but I don't think they'll be using that tank again."

Robespierre sat at Sister Marie's feet and waited to be pet.

"I don't think they'll find it for a while either. Jacob is erasing the tread marks as we speak."

The mayor of Brassac sighed. He never imagined that in fleeing Paris he would be forced to embrace a new universe of problems. If only there were someway to forget Nazis, nuns, and the war in general. Then, smiling at him from the other side of the road, he noticed Chloé Lapointe. He had seen her often when he was dating Noele, who was her longtime friend. In those days, he failed to notice how readily she laughed at his jokes or how subdued her congratulations was to the announcement of their engagement. He was not in Brassac, to see how Chloé reacted when Noele announced her candidacy to become a nun.

"René...bon matin!" she cried, waving enthusiastically.

He looked at her, not quite sure how to respond. There had been absolutely nothing good about the afternoon or the morning for that matter. There was nothing to indicate that tomorrow would be any better. Something had to be done. "Chloé, would you like to get a drink with me?"

Chloé stopped in her footsteps, taken aback by the unexpected suggestion. "Oui, but of course. Can I ask why?"

René looked her in the eye and remarked, "I should very much like to share the company of a beautiful French woman, and you are French, are you not?"

"Quite," she replied, blushing.

"I only ask that you not speak of things like the war or of Germans, because I should only like to remember happier days. I think if I should drink wine with a woman, such as you, perhaps I might remember them."

She really did not know what to think, but she delightedly took his arm and allowed him to escort her to wherever he might.

"Friedrich, you know our work here is very important. A subdued France is one that allows us to complete our good work in England, Russian and yes, one day, even America. The Füerer desires that France not provide yet another source of trouble." Klaus distrustfully eyed the townspeople that walked past them, seeing each one of them as a potential inconvenience. "If France were to become a problem it would, essentially, be the opening of another front. We must ensure that the resistance is cut off at its roots and before the weeds have time to spread throughout Europe. I hope I can count on you to aggressively stomp out anyone who would put our authority in question?"

"My captain, you know that I will not stop at anything to ensure that we bring glory to the fatherland." Friedrich wheezed in a way that suggested both excitement and asthma.

Klaus looked to where the tank tracks disappeared. "We will keep this particular matter to ourselves. We cannot let word get back to Berlin that, on our first day here, the resistance was able to steal a tank right from under our noses."

"Leave the matter to me," replied Friedrich. "I will find who is responsible and impress upon them the error of their ways."

"I know you will Friedrich. I know you will."

CHAPTER FIVE
STABBING AT THE TRUTH

"Nein, du dummkopf!" The German officer threw the orders at his subordinate. "Die sendung ist das reisen mit der bahn! Es ist sehr wichtig!"

Father Jubé paused nearby and pretended to read a notice. He had taken an interest in the increased German activity near Brassac. It was an old habit from his days in the army before he had become a chaplain. The words, "important shipment," in German, had caught his attention. He noticed one of the soldiers gestured towards him, but the superior officer sneered and said something about, "just a French priest," which he underlined with a dismissive wave. Little did they realize that Father Jubé had studied German, extensively, during the First World War.

"Your men need to be on the south side of the trestle," continued the officer. "Do you understand the location?"

"Near Brassac?"

"Yes, dummkopf. Tuesday at eleven p.m. Are we clear?"

"Ja! The Brassac rail depot."

"Not the rail depot...by the bridge. Here, look at the map. We're trying to be discreet. Without this munitions shipment, we might as well be carrying toy guns. You will not fail us?"

"No, sir." The obersoldat held the map, upside down and

nodded confidently.

The officer considered him with the regard he might provide a chimpanzee. "Why do I have the feeling I'll be visiting the northern front soon?"

Friedrich walked down the quaint country road and paused to look at the document Klaus had provided him with his dossier. There was a small black and white photo of the Vichy officer who had disappeared, as well as a diagram of the area in which he had last been observed. Little did he know that he stood mere steps from where Sister Dominique had delivered the fatal shot. There was not much to go on, but Friedrich prided himself on digging up information where others found, but a cold trail. He was not afraid to use methods that other National Socialists might find distasteful. At any rate, the small farm looked as good a place to start, as any. He approached the man who worked, industriously, on his knees; seemingly unaware of his presence. "What are you growing?"

Michel Mouyal looked up and was surprised to find a stout-looking German staring down at him. "Garlic," he replied. "It is popular in many of our local dishes."

Friedrich nodded, approvingly. "Is business good?"

"Terrible," Michel replied. "Perhaps, things will change?"

"You do not think things are getting better?" Friedrich protested. "Every morning, when I wake up, I ask myself what I can do to help my fellow man."

Michel wondered how he might have gone from tending his garden to a conversation on public service, with a Nazi. "Is there something I can help you with?"

Friedrich smiled. "Why...yes--"

"Monsieur Mouyal, but my friends call me Michel."

"How nice. There was a police officer that went missing a while back. Are you familiar with this?"

Michel wiped some of the sweat from his forehead, which was replaced with soil. "I heard about it, but very little."

The short German nodded, sympathetically. "It is very hot here, let us go talk under your porch?"

Michel agreed and led Friedrich over to his house. "The officer was a surly gentleman. He didn't have a lot of friends."

"Surely, you must suspect somebody? Local people talk, well...that has been my experience. There have been other, more recent, problems and I am in the problem-solving business."

Michel poured himself some water and offered a glass to his guest who, politely, refused.

"You see, being an outsider makes it very difficult for me to get the information I need to do my job. How can I help the people I have been assigned to if they cannot trust me enough to provide me the information I need to protect them?"

"I'm really sorry," repeated Michel. "I'm afraid there isn't anything else I have to offer."

Friedrich sighed, having concluded that a different strategy would be necessary. "This is my favorite dagger," he said, producing a finely crafted ornamental blade. I carry it with me at all times. It says 'Alles fur Deutchland,' which is how I try to live my life. I got it when I was a member of the Sturmabteilung. You might know us as the 'brown shirts?' Yes, I was quite busy on the night of the Long Knives, but I did not use this dagger. No, I'm afraid I'm not very good with it."

Michel was now certain he did not like the direction to which the conversation had pivoted. "If you will excuse me, I have my garden--"

Friedrich grabbed Michel and forced him to listen. "Let's play a game?" He pushed him against the wall. "You see, sometimes when I throw my dagger, it hits with the point of the blade and other times it hits with the handle. Look at all the scratches, such a shame. Let's see...I will ask you some questions and for every answer I don't like, I will throw my dagger? What do you think? Sounds fun?"

"I swear I don't know anything. Why can't you just leave me alone?" Michel's eyes wandered to a resting pitchfork, but Friedrich smiled in a way that made it clear he hoped he would try.

"Shall we play with my Luger? It's your choice?" Friedrich watched, approvingly, as Michel settled against the wall. It was a posture of resignation that he was familiar with from his victims. "First question. Who, in your neighborhood, objects to the German presence in France?"

Michel thought hard and truly desired to give an honest answer. "Everyone." The dagger whistled through the air, and the nickel butt end of the handle struck him in his gut. It knocked the wind out of him, and he doubled over.

"Wait," Friedrich reflected, as he collected the dagger from the ground. "I should have been more specific. That one is my fault. Please forgive me. I should have said, who in the area speaks the most, openly, of their dislike of Germany or Vichy? Please take your time."

Sweat poured from Michel's forehead and at a rate that exceeded working in his field. He wondered if the German realized that he had been openly critical of the new government and its collaboration with Germany? He knew he would have to provide some name, but he did not desire to bring trouble upon any man. Least of all, himself.

"Louis Blériot!" Michel cried, suddenly.

The dagger whizzed through the air, and its blade stuck in his shoulder. Friedrich walked over and pulled it out. "The French aviator? Now I *have* learned something. You do not see me as your friend, which is sad. I thought I had finally met somebody I could trust. That is why I like this game...I always learn so many things. Let's play again."

"I know who did it," cried Jacob, who unexpectedly appeared at the door.

"Monsieur Mouyal, I did not know you had a son! Please come out child. Your father and I are playing a game."

Jacob saw that blood seeped from his father's shoulder. "You want Philippe Gaumont. He hates Vichy...and Germany, especially."

Friedrich used Michel's water to clean the blade of his dagger. "Perhaps you are right, but your father and I were only getting started."

"Please go there and see for yourself," pleaded Jacob. He ran over and placed himself in front of his father.

"Yes, I will, but I think you will come along."

"Bless me father for I have sinned. My last confession was three hours ago."

"Very funny Marie. You know I didn't call you here for that." Father Jubé put his face close to the lattice. "I need your help and discretion is of the utmost importance."

"I don't know why you think I can't be discrete!" Sister Marie protested, loudly. People in the sanctuary turned to see who was yelling from inside the confessional booth.

Father Jubé tried to hush her, "Please just try harder than usual. People in this town often give you and the other sisters the benefit of the doubt, but Nazis are not so lenient."

Sister Marie sat up straight. "Nazis? What does this have to do with Nazis?"

"That's why you're here," he whispered. "There is to be an arms shipment coming to Brassac and I need you to see it never gets here."

"Why me? You were the soldier. What am I supposed to do?"

Father Jubé slid a piece of paper between a hole in the screen. "A couple weeks ago, a member of the French resistance came to confession. He had just killed a man."

"How dreadful!" cried Sister Marie. She could hear murmurs from outside the confessional.

"But that is not what he came to confess. He was sorry that the man had suffered. He had meant to shoot him in the head, but had missed...and punctured his neck."

Sister Marie unfolded the paper and saw that Father Jubé had drawn a map of the rail line with a key and a compass. "You wish me to give him this?"

"Yes, his name was Claude Delacroix. That has the location of where the train, with ammunition and other supplies, will be met. As you can see...it's not quite coming into Brassac." René adjusted his collar. "And there is a slight problem--"

"Yes?"

"I don't actually know where to find him. That's where you come in. People are used to you walking around, carrying a gun, and getting into mischief. You are less likely to raise suspicions than me. I rarely stray far from my office."

"What does he look like?"

"I didn't actually get a good look at him. He offered me his name, which I thought was unusual. I think he will not hesitate to do what is necessary to keep the Germans from tightening the noose around our necks. Can I count on you?"

"You know that I would do anything for you."

"Then I will pray for your success," he concluded, but Sister Marie's distinctive outline sat motionless. "Is there something else?"

"You didn't hear my confession yet," she protested.

"If this is about the tank, I already know it was you."

"Oh, I don't feel sorry about that."

"Then if it's about your feelings for me, again--"

"Oh, never mind," huffed Sister Marie as she stormed out of the confessional.

Father Jubé laughed, despite himself.

There was an intense rapping at the door. Sister Anette looked, searchingly, at Sister Beatrice and wondered if she should open it. It seemed too urgent to not be the sound of unexpected, and unwelcome, trouble. Beatrice glanced behind the curtains and indicated that it was safe to unlatch the lock. The door creaked open, and Monsieur Mouyal fell inside as if he had been resting against it.

"They've got my boy. Those Nazi bastards have taken him! You have got to help me!"

Sister Noele noticed his shirt, covered in blood. "You're bleeding! Please come in and lie down."

"We don't have time for that!" protested Michel. "For whatever reason, I know Jacob trusts you. I would have gone to the mayor--"

"René is flawed, but trustworthy," Sister Beatrice informed him.

"Maybe, but I don't have time to do a character evaluation and he keeps bad company. Anyway, my boy tells me you're not afraid to get your hands dirty. Will you help me or not?"

Sister Dominique threw rifles at Beatrice, Gabrielle, and Anette. "Let Sister Noele treat your wounds and we will do what we can. Where is he?"

"They're going to Philippe's house! When they get there, they'll know for sure Jacob lied." Michel lay on the bed and let Sister Noele clean the wound the dagger had made. Blood pattered, softly, onto the ground.

Empty bottles of Cabernet, Pinot Noir, and Bordeaux lay strewn about Philippe's lawn chair. Passed out at its center, an embarrassing spectacle for all to see, was Philippe; who snored violently, like a bear with allergies. He did not notice the unexpected guests who had let themselves in through his rotting fence. Nor was he aware that a short German held a dagger, but inches from his face. The sunlight reflected off the cheek of its blade and focused tightly upon his whiskers. Philippe smelled smoke and awoke to find his beard smoldering. "Ah, I'm on fire." He picked up a bottle and doused his face with wine.

"No, but thank you for the suggestion," replied Friedrich. "I am Friedrich, and this is--"

"I know who he is. What are you doing here? I haven't done anything."

"Well, that really is the issue. Apparently you are the main suspect in the disappearance of a police officer and other troubles that we have been having. I do not like troubles."

Philippe sobered up in record time. "Now listen; I am a supporter of Vichy. The French Republic was ridden with gout!" He put up a blistered hand. "I tried to join the Service d'ordre legionnaire."

"You tried to join the SOL? This I had not heard. Can you prove it?"

"Yes, let me go into my house and I will get the papers." Philippe looked at Jacob and began to piece together why he had accompanied the German. "Wait! Did he tell you that I was against Vichy? You do realize what he is? He is an undesirable...a Jew."

Friedrich considered Jacob anew, but he could tell by the look of fear, in the boy's eyes, that Philippe had been truthful. "Never mind the papers. That won't be necessary." He pointed at Jacob with the end of his dagger. "Is it possible that you have lied to me? You do know what that means? We shall have to continue the game I started with your father." He pushed him into Philippe's chair. It smelled of despair.

"Maybe we should wait for Sister Marie?" protested Sister Anette. Her tunic clung to the dress guard of her bicycle, and she peddled with all her might. "What if she disproves?"

65

"That's practically her calling," Sister Beatrice replied. "We only own four bicycles and there isn't time to form a quorum." They bounced along the muddy road towards Philippe's house; rifles slung over their backs. "She has been acting very peculiar lately, anyway."

"Didn't she say she was looking for someone?" asked Sister Anette. "Maybe, she needs our help?"

"Don't be such a ninny," replied Sister Gabrielle.

"What is our plan here, anyway? Are you going to shoot someone?" cried Anette.

"If I have to," replied Sister Dominique. "I haven't lost any sleep since the last time." Robespierre sat in the large basket attached to her handlebars, and his tongue flapped in the wind. He was too large and every time they hit a bump, he flew into the air.

"That's what concerns me," replied Sister Anette.

"Philippe, would you really like to be in the militia?" asked Friedrich. He looked at his pocket watch and realized that he only had another hour before he was due to meet up with Klaus, who valued punctuality more than investigations. Returning empty-handed, however, was simply not an option. He would, at the very least, need to be in the position to provide new information or have a potential lead.

"Of course," he replied. "The English bombed my cousins and I hate what France had become before you Germans arrived."

Friedrich nodded in sympathy with his sentiments. "I like to play a game. What I do is...I ask a question, and if I don't like the answer I throw this dagger. Would you have a problem with me playing this game?"

"War is a messy business," Philippe observed. It was clear, however, that he had yet to embrace his position.

"Yes, indeed it is. What if you played the game? Yes, I think that shall be the real test." He smiled in appreciation of his perverse efficiency, for he would kill two birds with one stone.

Philippe began to sweat. Although he barely knew Jacob, he was not interested in playing a game where he might have to stab the youth. Friedrich studied his eyes as he weighed the moral consequences. Finally, self-preservation overrode his conscience, and he allowed the dagger to be placed in the palm of his hand.

"First question," began Friedrich. "Does anyone in your family know about the missing police officer?"

Jacob looked about, to see what remained of his options. Fleeing would certainly mean getting a dagger in his back and expose his father to further danger. "No one knew him and that's all I know."

Friedrich took a moment to consider his answer. "What do

you think Philippe? Was that a good response?"

The dagger was slippery in Philippe's nervous palm. "I think it was. He's just an enfant--"

Now a look of disappointment spread across Friedrich's face. "Philippe...and I was just beginning to trust you, but now I'm not so sure. How to find out if you are as enthusiastic a supporter of the new order, as you claim--" He seemed to grapple with the dilemma, but then reached a decisive conclusion. "Throw it."

Philippe raised the dagger, which shook from both his nerves and the alcohol that lingered in his system. As he prepared to release the blade, there was a loud *crack,* and it flew from his hand. Friedrich comprehended the sound, immediately, and dove behind a bushel of hay.

Jacob recognized his opportunity and reached for a discarded wine bottle, which he brought down upon Friedrich's head. He took off into the hedges, opposite of the direction from where the flash had originated. He found his escape, remarkably easy, as Philippe just sat on the ground with his hands over his head and shook.

CHAPTER SIX
THE MAQUISARD

Claude Delacroix cast an uneasy eye from behind the overgrowth, aware that stealth was as much about restricting his movement as preserving his coverage. He withdrew his pistol, scarred from a lifetime of field time and a multitude of adventures. Its leather holster had been a gift from his late wife and originally it had been a light-tan, but after many a spring rain it had matured into a deep mahogany. Claude had concluded the weathering was actually an improvement, and he treasured it, being deeply sentimental. At moments such as this, he longed for a Welrod pistol which was far quieter and better suited for such delicate work. He figured if he were a member of the resistance in Normandy or Paris, he might find himself so equipped. Claude had to make due with what equipment he could find, which usually meant appropriating whatever the Germans weren't watching. Anyhow, the Ruby pistol had been his trusted sidearm in the First World War, and it carried nine shots; a technical point that had saved him on more than one occasion in the trenches. He had used it for so long that it had, practically, become an extension of his arm. Wherever Claude was able to look, it faithfully placed a dot of lead. Now he searched for a clear view of the German, but the child had knocked them flat to the ground, with an empty bottle of

Chenin Blanc. The loud *thunk* it made caused him to wince, both in response to how it must have felt and from the realization that the Nazi would now be safely spread out, behind cover.

He had, covertly, followed the pair for the last hour. His suspicions were, naturally, raised at the sight of a ten-year-old boy leading a jackbooted Nazi down their idyllic country road. *Well, this isn't something you see everyday*, he thought. He trailed them, from just out of sight until they found themselves at Philippe's house. Claude was not acquainted with the drunkard though, having only recently relocated to the Tarn department. It was plainly obvious, however, that the German must be on a fact-finding mission and looking for information on any members of the local resistance. This was quite problematic, as he *was* the local resistance. At any rate, the Germans had not come to the area to enjoy the local cuisine.

Claude's first encounter, with his neighbors to the north, had occurred when he was just sixteen. Too young to enlist, in the First World War, he had simply stolen a uniform off a fallen French private and lied that he had been separated from his unit. There had never been enough time to contradict his story, as the war came to an end two months later. During those sixty days, not unlike Orpehus, he went to Hell and back. Upon looking into his eyes and seeing the horrors reflected there, no one further questioned his age.

When Hitler invaded France, Claude understood well his reasons. He was just as anxious to revisit past differences. This time, however, it would not be as a member of the French Army. No, too many of them were now collaborators and traitors. Many of the rest were in exile. The resistance remained his best recourse to punish the Krauts for having stolen his childhood.

Now, as a man, he looked back with those same troubled eyes. He watched, as the Hun made the young boy sit in a chair with nothing, but fear to bind him. The drunken Frenchman seemed complicit and even received a dagger from the German. Claude was so surprised, when he lifted the blade, that he almost forgot to shoot. The boy did his part by soundly striking the German, but Claude would very much like to have placed another shot, right upon the swastika that ornamented his peak cap. It was never wise, however, to tarry once your location was compromised. He sighed in frustration and quietly slipped away.

Sister Marie had expected to be the bearer of news, but she returned home to find herself in need of further illumination. Michel Mouyal rested on one of their beds. His face was milky white; as if prepared for a mimodrama. Although not a member of their parish, Sister Marie knew everyone within ten kilometers.

71

Noele threw a bloody rag, into a small pail, and looked up to discover that Marie had returned. "Hell's bells...where have you been?" She retrieved a clean towel and pressed it hard against Michel's shoulder.

"I've been searching for someone for Father Jubé. What in heaven's name happened? Where are the others?"

"They went to find Jacob. A German stabbed Monsieur Moyal and took him!"

Marie looked at Michel and saw that he seemed to be stable and in good hands. "Where did they go?"

"Monsieur Philippe's," grunted Michel.

Marie shook as she grabbed her rifle. "I'll be back in an hour." She would table her fears, for the meantime.

Monsieur Moyal took the rag and waved Noele off. "I'll be fine. Please...go help my boy!"

"I'm coming with you," Noele yelled, as she ran after her. Sister Marie was outside looking, frantically, for their bicycles. "The other sisters already took them."

They ran down the back alley and hoped to God that they might find a couple more that they could borrow. Then Sister Marie noticed Klaus' Škoda Kfz. 21 cabriolet, sitting forsaken and unattended.

Friedrich's blurry eyes struggled to focus, and he was aware of a pounding sensation; like someone had been given the command to beat his head to quarters. How much time had passed? Maybe only seconds, but for all he knew, it might have been years. There was the stench of wine, as could only be fermented within a drunkard's mouth. Friedrich became aware of Philippe, who was practically in his face, just as he was slapped. The smack startled him into cognition because he struck him back. "Don't touch me you filthy Frenchman."

"Sorry, sir. They're getting away."

This registered because Friedrich stood up and ran, only to nearly fall; as dizziness superseded his will. He used the inertia to push himself forward and onto the road.

"You're going the wrong way," Philippe protested.

Friedrich went opposite from Jacob's escape route, but as luck so often benefits the wicked, he happened upon the nuns riding their bicycles. "Halt!" he shouted, in his most authoritarian voice. Seeing no response to his instruction, he pulled out his pistol and fired into the air. The bikes skidded to a stop, and its riders turned around to see who had demanded their attention. Friedrich casually strode up to them, still wincing from the pain of the bottle that had struck him. "Hello, ladies. You seem to be in quite a hurry."

Sister Anette smiled and replied, "We're hunting."

"Oh, I'm quite sure, but what are you after, that is the question?" He looked at their rifles with professional interest. "Lebel rifles. Not as good as German, but able to accomplish an accurate shot from a suitable distance." He grabbed the barrel of Sister Anette's rifle, but it was cold. A look of disappointment spread over his face. "You know, I wonder if it is not coincidence that you are here?" He placed his hand on Sister Beatrice's rifle, but it had also not been fired recently. "Isn't it odd that nuns are riding around on such a day, with firearms strapped to their backs? You are nuns?" He grabbed Sister Gabrielle's Lebel, but it was, likewise, cool. He approached Sister Dominique's bicycle, and Robespierre began to growl. "I think I am about to uncover this mystery." He grabbed her gun's barrel and was surprised to find that it was frigid.

"We're just looking for quail," replied Sister Beatrice. "Not that they haven't probably been scared away by now."

Friedrich took Beatrice's rifle and unloaded it on the ground. "So, you have not heard of the order for those in the formally unoccupied areas to surrender their hunting rifles?"

"What are you talking about?" Sister Gabrielle grunted and embraced her Lebel.

Sister Beatrice was alarmed, for entirely different reasons. "We have heard no such thing!"

"Yes, I'm afraid I shall have to confiscate them." Friedrich received the rifles from the rest of them. "Do not think me unkind. The actual punishment is death, but executing a group of nuns would hardly help the image of the Wehrmacht or the Gestapo."

Sister Dominique, not known for her sense of restraint, mocked, "Well, you certainly wouldn't want us hurting your reputation."

Friedrich was not sure if it was the nuns or the blow from the bottle, which prolonged his headache. Please be sure to surrender any other weapons you might have, immediately."

Sister Noele pretended to enjoy the midday sun while she looked for signs of any Germans who might be out and about. Sister Marie, who had experience in such matters, worked on starting the car; from further down the street. If the Gestapo should appear, she was to sneeze loudly and try to engage them in light conversation until Sister Marie could escape. Time, however, was of the essence.

Across the street was Chez Honoré, a small family restaurant with three tables and two sun-damaged umbrellas. Known for its rabbit and sausage cassoulet, the cuisine already attracted a steady clientele of German officers. Fortunately, none of them seemed presently about, but Noele wondered if any of the Nazis that hung around Brassac, might be inside enjoying an afternoon meal. Then she noticed a face that filled her, equally, with dread.

Enjoying a leisurely afternoon lunch, at one of Chez Honoré's quaint outside tables, was her former fiancée; the current mayor of Brassac. He had the wide-eyed expression he wore when he told, what he felt was, a particularly witty joke. It was difficult to hear from across the road, but then her ears recognized yet another familiar cadence. It was the easy laughter that came from someone trying to put their date at ease. The laugh was long-familiar because it came from her childhood friend Chloé, dressed in finery that failed to reflect that Europe was embroiled in war or that France was under occupation. She touched René's hand and wiped her eyes as if his observations were so amusing they had driven her to tears.

Noele remembered what Sister Marie had told her, when she began her candidacy to become a nun, "The essence of love is self-denial. I never understood what that meant until I became a nun. I denied myself for Francis, and he denied himself for God. Unless you learn to release everything you hold dear...you will never, truly, embrace anything."

She had not yet even been allowed to enter the novitiate phase. Perhaps Sister Marie could only view her from the reflection of her own heartbreak? Now as Noele watched René and seethed in her jealousy, she wondered if Sister Marie had been sagacious to hold her back? If her former self, could yet be summoned like Samuel's ghost, was she truly ready to join the other sisters?

René looked up to discover Sister Noele glaring at him from across the road. Being on a date was awkward enough without having a nun's icy stare bearing down on you. Having a nun, that used to be your fiancée, looking through you, with their well-practiced, judgmental gaze, practically constituted a psychological attack. He took a long gulp of wine and cleared his throat. He asked Chloé an inconsequential question to keep her attention directed away from the source of his discomfort.

"And what about you," asked Chloé. "Surely you have many responsibilities now that you're mayor? It must be so exciting and who knows where it will take you?" She made no attempt to veil her flirting.

"I should very much like to have remained the village carpenter, but no one has the time or income for such frivolities now. What better responsibility could there be than to make people happy with your craftsmanship?"

Chloé looked at him as if he was joking. "But don't be so modest. You represent all of us, and it is to you that the Germans come when they have a problem."

"Why should I want Germans bringing me problems?" René looked up and saw that Sister Noele had disappeared. "Now, let's not speak of my work. Why, this is almost like being in Paris!"

"Almost?" Chloé wondered. She had never been to Paris, but hardly a day went by that she did not dream about it.

"Yes, well the company is certainly on par." René looked up and watched as Klaus' staff car whizzed by with Sister Marie at the wheel and Sister Noele riding shotgun.

"René, you have hardly touched your Navarin D'Agneau and the spring vegetables are so delightful."

"Suddenly, I'm not hungry," he replied, throwing down his fork.

Chloé looked at his maudlin expression and wondered if she had ruined his appetite. "You know René, I never truly noticed you before you were mayor, but something about the way you control the town--"

"I appear to be in control?" he stammered.

"Oh, yes," she cooed.

"What a relief."

Sister Marie's hunch that the owner of the Škoda cabriolet had been in the restaurant was an educated one. Uniformed Germans had been observed there, in the late afternoon. Had she seen René, with Chloé, she would never have placed Noele at that spot alone, what with their complex history. It was, however, a safe bet that the cabriolet's owner would soon reveal himself.

As if on cue, Klaus exited the restaurant, genuinely, seeming to have reconciled himself to life in provincial France. "Monsieur Honoré, your Boeuf Bourguignon is a revelation." The opportunity for advancement in his new assignment was miniscule, but the food was quite agreeable. As he turned to depart, he saw René sitting with a beautiful, young lady. "Monsieur Mayor, I did not know that you were here and what lovely company you have."

Chloé blushed and found herself quite taken with the imperial-looking German. His finely pressed uniform appeared very smart to her aesthetic sensibilities. René, temporarily, achieved translucence to her.

"Where is Friedrich? Were you dining alone?" René asked, more interested to make conversation than determine if anything was amiss.

"Well, he was supposed to meet me, but he never showed. He must be quite engaged in his work?" Klaus had enjoyed his meal so much, that he hadn't given Friedrich's whereabouts any thought. "This reminds me; we should meet tomorrow to discuss some of the matters that have arisen as a result of the change of status of the free territories."

"But, of course," René replied. "Does nine o'clock sound agreeable?"

"Nine it is," Klaus confirmed and kissed Chloé's hand. "Ma chérie...such a pleasure." He took out the keys to his car and departed with the euphoria that comes from a perfect afternoon meal. Yes, he was starting to like his new assignment and the countryside agreed with him more than he cared to admit.

Klaus reached the end of town, but had still not arrived at his automobile. Perhaps, he thought, he should have made a left when he turned right? Then he noticed a small pool of oil. It was the unmistakable mark that his Škoda left wherever it was parked. Now, he was filled with the dreadful realization that his car had, indeed, been stolen.

Friedrich waited impatiently for Philippe to complete his search of the Mouyal farm. He was not afraid to get his hands dirty, but the thought of riffling through a family of undesirable's personal effects, was best left to others. At last, Philippe exited the farmhouse with a bewildered look that made clear they had returned to find the property vacant. Friedrich twirled his dagger and sighed. "Monsieur Mouyal did not wait to conclude our game? That is very rude."

"The child did not return home. I looked everywhere." Philippe was willing to assist the Nazi, but he was also relieved to not be a party to his methods.

"I am not surprised," Friedrich concluded. "People have so little respect for authority these days. Oh well, as of this moment, the Mouyal family has been officially denaturalized. You may burn their house."

Philippe made a grunt that reflected how perplexed he was at the suggestion. "Isn't that a waste? This is a perfectly good home."

"The lesson, itself, is a better use of resources than an old farmhouse." He was starting to lose patience with his recently recruited collaborator. The quality of native partners, in the province, was certainly below par.

"Still, to burn another man's home--" Philippe looked at its attractive stone walls and whimsically painted windows. He remembered the fine potbelly stove he had seen inside.

"Are you sure you want to be a member of the Service d'ordre legionnaire?"

"But, of course."

"What if I were to tell you that all of his land was about to be redistributed to you?" Friedrich waited for Philippe's greed to help him overcome any moral reservations.

"I think we can use this hay and these kerosene lanterns..." Philippe began to stack fuel around the base of the building, but because it was made of stone, it just charred the granite.

"I am already late," complained Friedrich, who tossed a lantern through one of the windows. It broke apart and quickly caught the interior of the house on fire. He stepped back to shield himself from the smoke. "Must we Germans do everything?"

"Must you Germans do anything?" Philippe whispered to himself. Above the roar of the fire, he knew that Friedrich would not hear him.

Sister Beatrice pedaled her bicycle for all she was worth, but then lifted her feet to allow the pedals to turn about on their own. "Look sisters! The German's car!"

"Quick...hide!" croaked Gabrielle.

"No, he's already seen us," Beatrice replied. "Pedal slow and act natural."

"How do we do that?" wondered Sister Dominique.

"Be nun-like, but not how you normally act."

The Škoda cabriolet pulled up to reveal Sister Marie and Noele, who appeared every bit like they were out for a Sunday drive.

"Good Lord...what are you doing with that car?" stammered Sister Beatrice. "What if somebody saw you?"

"I'll worry about that later," replied Sister Marie. "Were you coming from Philippe's?"

"Yes, Jacob was there, but he must have escaped. Someone helped him, but we aren't sure who? The short German took all our rifles. Apparently, they're illegal now."

"Well, ours are in the backseat of this stolen Nazi staff car. I'm guessing that's frowned upon. We best dispose of this thing. Sister Nicole and I will meet you back home. There's a good chance he went there."

"Is that smoke?" asked Sister Noele. "It looks like it's coming from the Mouyal farm."

"We'll go there first. See you in a while."

"I doubt anyone is there," replied Sister Beatrice.

Sister Marie had already gunned the engine and taken off, leaving the others to cough from the smoke and the dust.

"Forgive me father for I have sinned. It has been five days since my last confession."

Father Jubé looked through the screen. "What did you steal this time Léon?"

Léon's life of petty crime had started at a very young age. It all began with a chocolate croissant that he had spied at Monsieur Louvel's boulangerie. His mother had been quite quick to dismiss him when he pointed to it, excitedly, as it danced like a chocolate-covered crescent moon within the circles of his eyes. Powdered sugar filled its creases and folds while ganache poured from its buttery ends. Then, a miracle. His mother dropped some coins and ever the gentleman; Monsieur Louvel bent over to help her retrieve it. Léon snatched the croissant and quickly hid it in his corduroy jacket. If the taste had not been so sweet, or if his mother had not been so frugal, perhaps he might not have embarked upon a life of larceny. Even now, in his twenties, stealing from bakeries remained the primary staple of his criminal career.

It was not that Léon was without scruples. He attended Mass regularly and confessed to Father Jubé, a careful rundown of his various exploits. It had become a regular part of his routine to return to the scene of his crimes, to pay for any transgressions. Shopkeepers in the area simply expected it as a natural part of the transaction. They did not even bother to guard themselves against future indiscretions as they knew Léon would surely return, at Father Jubé's direction, to make amends.

Léon looked down in shame. "You know me so very well. It is as if our Heavenly Father has opened my heart to you and laid bare my faults."

"You're far too predictable to require divine help. What was it this time?" The priest smiled from the other side of the confessional. He was, particularly, fond of this parishioner.

"A German mine. Forgive me father, but it was just lying there, and it was so beautiful and spherical."

"Antitank or personnel? Does it look like a can or a plate?" Léon now had Father Jubé's complete attention."

The thief was far too trusting to question the priest's interest in artillery. "I don't know...like a plate with a handle."

Father Jubé placed the palms of his hands together and appeared lost in thought. "Antitank...a Teller mine, I think. Léon, I'm concerned that you could get hurt."

"If they catch me?"

"No, you're far too clever to get caught...from the mine. I had better take it to keep you safe. I was in the army once, you know?"

"Yes, I see what you mean." Léon teared up. "I am truly sorry. How many Our Fathers and Hail Marys should I say?"

"I think it might be better if you used your efforts to find some German rifles, maybe some Gewehr 1888s."

"Are you quite sure?"

"Of course I'm sure...I'm a priest. Can you find some grenades, as well?"

Marie and Noele pulled up to the Mouyal farm and found nothing but smoldering granite stones and charcoaled beams of hand-hewn wood. The remains of a potbelly stove stood defiantly in the middle, untouched. Sister Marie's anger moistened eyes burned, and her hand gripped her rifle.

"I doubt anyone is here," Noele concluded. "We should get

rid of the car before we're spotted."

Sister Marie was in no mood for helpful observations. She honestly hoped someone came back, so she could show them what she thought of their handiwork. "Ouais, I know just the place to put it and then we'll walk back on foot."

There was a small tap on the door, but when Sister Beatrice opened it she found nothing, but air. Again, she heard something small hit the window, but behind the drapes she only found darkness.

"What is it?" asked Sister Anette.

"I don't know. There's no one there." She was interrupted by another *clink* against the glass. "All right, if anyone--" This time, a small hand waved from within the bushes. She looked around to make sure no one watched and casually strolled over. "Jacob, is that you child?"

"Is my father in there?" he asked.

"Yes, come with me," she lifted the front of her dress for him to hide under.

"I'm pretty sure that's not kosher," he replied.

"Do you want to sleep inside where it's warm...or out here tonight?"

Jacob sighed, and crouch walked under her habit, as they made their way back to the door.

"Did you find anything?" asked Sister Dominique.

"Just this," Sister Beatrice replied, lifting her dress to reveal Jacob.

"My son!" cried Michel. "You found my boy!" He groaned from the pain, as Jacob embraced him. "Don't worry, I'll be fine. The bleeding isn't getting any worse."

There was a knock on the back door.

"Who is it this time?" Sister Anette walked to the back and found Marie and Noele, sopping wet. "We're going to need more towels."

Father Jubé arrived, and over the next hour they determined the best course of action, to ensure that the Mouyal family would be safe for the remainder of the war. "There is a family in Moissac, who used to live here. I taught their children. They have written me, and I have learned that many others, who have been denaturalized, have taken refuge there. The town protects them, and I am sure they will look after you."

"I do not know how we can thank you," replied Michel.

Sister Marie scoffed. "If this war is won, it won't be because of guns or weapons. Violence may be the battle, but conscience *is* the war." She stuffed a map into Michel's hands. "Travel at night and send word when you have safely arrived."

"One of the families has a two-way radio you can use to contact us," added Father Jubé. "Speak only in the provided code."

Sister Anette handed them a bag with a wedge of Brie and some bread. They watched silently as they slipped out the back door. As soon as the pair had left, they dropped to their knees and prayed for their safety.

Philippe and Friedrich followed the tracks of the Škoda until it led them to a small pond, just outside of Brassac. Its shallows were a clutter of reeds, rushes, and delicate waterlilies. Algae blooms kept its waters cloudy and secret.

"Well?" yelled Friedrich.

Philippe, who was waist high in water, poked around with a large stick. "Nothing yet...please, I am looking."

Then, Friedrich noticed a reflection in the water as the sun reflected off of something metallic, beneath the bluish-green algae. "Wait, I am seeing something." He entered the pond and sloshed over to where the water shimmered.

"No...wait, there is something solid. I have found it over here!" Philippe insisted.

The Nazi was not at all pleased at having been corrected by an inebriated Frenchman. "You are twenty meters from me. How can it be both here and there? It cannot be all these places!"

"Sorry, never mind...this is a tank." Philippe stood upon its submerged turret, appearing to hover in the middle of the pond.

"And this is the Škoda," replied Friedrich, seeing that the sun had reflected off of a mirror. "Someone is going to die a very slow and Germanic death."

CHAPTER SEVEN
VIVE LA RESISTANCE!

"Klaus...wherever is your car?" René could not help, but be astonished to see the image-conscious German officer pull up, to his office, in a putrid-green Kübelwagen. It rather resembled an upside down bathtub on wheels. With the spare tire, attached to its flattened hood, it looked like it had already been in an accident and pieces of the other car still lingered.

"It's been giving me trouble," he replied, nonchalantly, in an attempt to brush aside the indignity of his arrival. "I've been thinking of getting a new one."

René feigned being helpful. "Maybe something French, like a Citroën, as a display of goodwill?"

"Yes, an astute point," the German agreed and wondered if such an automobile might attract less ill-sentiment. "You have quite the political mind, but that is to be expected."

"So it would appear." The mayor wondered what Klaus would think if he knew how little experience in politics, he actually had. He very much preferred the old days, when he was his own boss. Working for others meant not being able to choose with whom he wished to associate. Being part of an organization meant appearing polite, as you watched stupidity become policy and accepted idiocy as the new norm. As he smiled, he thought of childhood friends and family, whom he longed to survive the war. If dealing with Hell's bureaucrats increased the odds of that goal being achieved, then he was prepared to take tea with the devil himself. He wondered however if it had placed him on the path to collaboration?

"You know, my trusted associate ran into some of your local clergy," Klaus took note of the recognition, and frustration, on the mayor's face.

"Did they really?" René immediately reached for his liquor cabinet.

"Yes, a group of nuns. Very colorful characters."

René poured the whiskey so fast that it spilled over his glass, but he took the shot anyway. "You don't say?"

Klaus removed his gloves. "Interestingly enough, they were all armed with Lebel rifles.

"Well, I suppose it starts with rulers and the next thing you know...that's just not enough anymore." He was not surprised that his German counterpart found his attempt at humor lacking. "Well, I'm sure they have the necessary hunting permits and when we were not occupied, the Lebel 1886 was a model not even required to be registered."

"See that is why I am here," replied Klaus. "I know that such news is often not easily disseminated in the countryside. I am giving the people in my administrative region until the end of the month to surrender their hunting rifles and ammunition. We had quite a bit of difficulty in the non-Vichy territories. Farmers hid their rifles in hay under floorboards, even with a death penalty. In Paris, we collected twelve truckloads of pistols and hunting rifles."

"That's quite remarkable," replied René, quick to pour himself another drink.

Klaus had hoped that the mayor would offer his assistance, but since he only seemed interested in numbing the impact of his visit, he cut to the chase. "As mayor, it is your responsibility to see that all firearms in this, formerly, unoccupied territory are collected and destroyed. The punishment for anyone who fails to comply with the order is, naturally, death. Do you think you can distribute this information immediately?"

René knew that the local farmers and hunters would not respond well to such an edict, but there was only one appropriate answer to such a leading question. "Yes...of course. Thank you for providing my countrymen with the time to comply."

"René, I am only here to help," replied Klaus. He reached across the table and took the bottle out of René's hand, to pour himself a drink.

It unnerved René to have the Nazi refer to him in such a familiar and casual manner. It made him consider whether such a close association with evil, was a poor reflection of his character. He wondered if it was even possible to retain one's scruples, in such times?

Within the shadows, Léon watched the three field-gray soldiers, who sat around a meager fire, not far from their Kfz. 70 personnel car. They seemed to be having a very good time, laughing and telling off-color jokes; in German. The only problem was that their rifles, the very Gewehr 1888s that Father Jubé had requested, lay within reach of their well-trained hands.

He crept towards the camp and made a professional assessment of the degree of risk associated with the determined act of larceny. Léon was not, entirely, sure what the priest had in mind; involving him in such intrigues. He only knew that Father Jubé was the man he aspired to be, but lacked the discipline to become.

"Morality is not black and white, but so preposterously complex that it springs forth from the mind of God," the priest had instructed him. "It is like a symphony that just one wrong note can destroy. Why are we so quick to attempt to rewrite its beauty?" War itself, though, was a bleak requiem, but for all its evils it had given Léon a chance at redemption.

Suddenly, Léon understood the priest's plan. Perhaps, in a freewill universe, God had no choice, but to make use of his imperfections? Certainly, on this day, as he stealthily approached the German camp Léon saw not a chance for thievery, but an opportunity for sanctification.

Léon searched around until he found what he had been looking for, a tree branch of his approximate size. He used his pocket knife to carefully slice a bushy section of it free. Lying on his back, he draped its leaves over him so that he appeared a component of the forest floor. When he had successfully slid underneath their car, he used his knife to cut each of the brake lines. He grabbed the frame of the vehicle, pushed it forward, and relied on inertia to send it barreling down the hill.

The soldiers looked up to see their car gain speed, as it raced down the incline, completely out of control. They did not even notice Léon, who lay still under his makeshift camouflage. As they ran after their car, they yelled salty accusations at each other so that Léon had to bite his lip to keep from laughing. He waited until they were out of sight and then simply stood, dropped the branch, and sauntered towards their campsite. Rifles, and other items that he felt might prove useful, now disappeared, until he heard the loud *crash* of the vehicle as it smashed into a gathering of trees at the bottom of the hill. Yes, if God could make use of Moses, who had once killed a man, perhaps there was a place for him?

"I hated the Nazis before, but now that they've taken my Lebel rifle--" Sister Dominique fumed and her dog Robespierre attempted to channel her anger, by chewing apart the drapes.

"Can you please control that dog of yours?" Sister Marie requested politely. It was not out of vanity, as they had long ago been made into ribbons. "And don't hate."

Sister Beatrice sighed, "Well, it was bound to happen. I suppose we will have to find other ways to put food on the table."

"Do we really have to eat salad day and night," complained Noele. "I want to eat at Chez Honoré."

Sister Marie saw an opportunity to instruct their young candidate, "Sacrifice is our vocation. We did not become nuns to live a life of luxury, but of service."

"Yes, mother superior," Noele replied, dutifully.

Sister Marie waited until the other sisters had settled. "I suppose now is as good a time, as any, to tell you. Father Jubé made a rather unconventional request of me, recently."

"And you gave into your basest desires?" Sister Anette asked, bluntly.

"Not that type of request!" Marie was more patient with Anette than the others were. "He asked me to find a member of the resistance. Unfortunately I failed, and I only had until tonight."

Sister Beatrice put down her copy of Dante's *Inferno*. "Why did he need you to find them in such a hurry?"

Marie took out the map Father Jubé had given her. "There is a train bringing arms to the German soldiers that have been repositioned to our area. I think we've all seen them around lately? Without those arms, it will be difficult for them to control us."

"Please," replied Dominique. "It would take more than guns."

Sister Marie was sure that there were many who would agree. "The way I see it, we only have to delay them long enough until the Americans and Brits can liberate us. Father Jubé had hoped this man...Claude would destroy the bridge. What happened to the Mouyal family is only the beginning, I'm afraid."

"This is true," agreed Noele. "I have heard stories from Paris and Bordeaux."

"But what can we do to stop them?" wondered Sister Beatrice. "If the army couldn't stop them, how can we?"

Sister Marie pulled the anti-tank mine out from under her bed. "Father Jubé gave this to me in case I found this...Claude Delacroix. I wonder if it might still be of use?"

There was a pregnant moment of silence, from the shock of seeing such a dangerous device in their home. Then Sister Anette and Noele began to laugh. It was a reaction to the absurdity of the situation and not from amusement.

"I don't see what's funny," replied Marie.

"Do you think we'd even know what to do with that?" replied Sister Beatrice, who examined it with her reading glasses. "Not to mention they took our rifles?"

Sister Dominique went to the closet and produced a bow, "Well, there's always the medieval approach." She seemed very eager at the thought. Archery was a regular activity at their school, and she was the primary instructor. Sister Marie had been in the position, on a number of occasions, of asking her not to use human-shaped silhouettes, as targets. Especially, after Father Jubé caught her congratulating one of the children on their "head shot."

Noele was not happy that the idea was even being given a fair hearing. "We don't know the first thing about blowing up a bridge...what if somebody got hurt?"

"She's right, you realize? Even I know that a land mine needs pressure to explode. There will be people on that train." Sister Beatrice had never imagined that being a nun would ever put her within arms length of such a dilemma.

Sister Marie sighed. "This is a serious matter to weigh. If only there were time to find this Claude fellow, but the central question is whether or not it is more loving to blow up that bridge or to simply let the weapons pass?" She was deeply conflicted, but whenever she found herself in such a position, her inclination was to act and then sort out her feelings later. She knew that this time, though, she would have to parse the moral consequences. "Well...it's not a civilian train and what would people think of us if we did nothing? Then we would be judged as complicit though it means going against our vows. We've already seen how war delights in leaving you with nothing, but the options that violate your principles. It is a peculiar form of wickedness."

Sister Dominique was less conflicted. "We know where they're going and we've got the way to stop it."

Sister Gabrielle never shirked from danger, no matter how large. "Those weapons *are* for controlling our students and their families--"

Sister Marie's eyes welled, with frustration from her predicament. "People always ask me, 'Why is there so much suffering in the world?' How do you explain the complications of freewill to someone that's in pain?" She clutched her rosary until her palm was embossed with its form. "I've begun to wonder...perhaps, it is not that God is cruel, but that we are indifferent?"

"Indifference is a well that never runs dry," agreed Sister Beatrice, "and as good a word for evil as was ever composed,"

Sister Marie huddled them close and whispered, but her voice was electric. "One day, no doubt, some of our own will be found guilty of such a sin...but let it not be the whole of the story."

"Then let's do it," replied Sister Dominique. "Let's blow up that bridge."

Father Jubé recognized the particular knock on his door, as being the one he had given Léon. It was the first two measures of, The Song of the Partisans. "Come in Léon, what do you have for me?"

Léon looked out the window, to confirm that he had not been followed. He opened his trench coat to reveal three rifles and four hand grenades.

"You did very well tonight," observed Father Jubé. He helped, carefully, remove the weapons from around Léon's person. The priest opened the closet door, hidden behind the bookshelf, and the rifles joined two other French guns that Marie had returned for safe keeping. "Thank goodness, you found these. Most of the ammunition we have are M/88 cartridges, which are no good for the Lebels." He admired a grenade that Léon had acquired and set it in the corner. "We'd better keep this away from Robespierre."

"Where ever did you get so much ammunition," marveled Léon, admiring the stacks of cartridges.

"You know you're not the only sinner in Brassac...just my favorite," replied Father Jubé with a smile.

"Oh!" Léon remembered and produced a rather smooshed croissant. Seeing Father Jubé's skeptical look, he added, "Don't worry...I'll pay for it."

The priest continued to glare, nonplussed.

"Tomorrow."

Then, with the tension of cracking ice, there was another knock on the door.

"Are you expecting anyone?" Léon wheezed, as they concealed their secret behind the bookcase.

"Don't worry. It's probably just one of the sisters," Father Jubé reassured him. "Go ahead and open it."

René stood at the door, removing his felt fedora. "Léon, how are you this evening?" He looked to where Francis sat, "Father, I am sorry if you are occupied with matters of a spiritual nature." He was well aware that Léon was in regular need of the priest's services.

"We had just finished," he replied, accommodatingly. "Please, won't you come in?"

René took a seat, but did not waste time with pleasantries. "Father, it's late so I will be direct with you. I know that you provide the nuns with the ammunition for their sport."

"This is not a secret," the priest replied, amicably.

"Yes, but I want to keep you out of trouble. I find myself in a most difficult position." René had known Father Jubé since he was, but a boy at his school. It was awkward to be in the position of laying down rules for the one who had disciplined him. The priest had instructed him in his catechism classes, in a manner, not unlike how Socrates had taught his students. "You see, the Germans have outlawed even old hunting rifles. Come tomorrow,

I will be in charge of disseminating this information."

"I see. That is not surprising."

"This community needs its institutions if there is to be any sense of normalcy and I value your role."

"Merci beaucoup," he replied, gratefully. He noticed a book missing on one of the shelves, that hid the closet, but casually replaced it before René could take notice.

"I don't want anything directing undue attention towards you or the nuns. Brassac needs its church and its school--" René tried to find a way to impress his concerns, without verbalizing them specifically. "The Germans don't seem interested in church affairs and I'd like to keep it that way.

"They would be fools to have interfered on their way up, but now that they are here...I do not expect such restraint to continue. Already hundreds of clergy have been imprisoned, an indication of their true intent." René was now the mayor, but he still appeared a naive schoolboy, to him. Still, Father Jubé knew that he was only trying to help. "René...mayor, I appreciate your concern." He reached into his desk and produced four boxes of ammunition, which he soundly placed on his desk.

René sighed, appreciatively. "Thank you for your cooperation. You cannot imagine how difficult this is for me."

"But, of course," Father Jubé replied, sympathetically.

The mayor noticed that Léon was acting even more cagey than

normal. "You don't have anything...do you, Léon?"

"Oh no," he sniveled. "I've given all mine away."

Claude, carefully, walked along the wooden trestle and searched for the perfect place to sabotage the railway. The waxing, gibbous moon provided him with modest cover, but he knew he needed to work quickly, as the train would not be long before its arrival. The timber would be no match for the grenades he had brought, and because the trestle was not intended to be a permanent structure, every pier was dependent on the next. The local medieval bridges were made out of stone and much more resistant to damage. His goal was only to derail the train, and the manner in which he had decided to accomplish this feat was very elementary. He fastened three grenades to the railway track, which he planned to activate with a string from the safe side of the trestle. He used butcher's twine to fasten the explosives and then tied another around a grenade's safety. It was not an elegant solution, but Claude had neither the resources nor experience to construct anything more elaborate. Satisfied, he grabbed his end and prepared to leave.

"Don't move," said an authoritative voice. "Not even to adjust that Basque beret."

Claude knew better than to reach for his pistol, when he had been caught red-handed. He thought about pulling the string, which would, at least complete his mission, and prevent the train from reaching its destination. He calculated whether the ravine, below the trestle, had enough water to cushion his fall, should he jump. Claude had escaped worse predicaments before. Better, though, he thought, to see if fortune smiled upon him enough to be able to fight again.

"What are you doing here?" pressed another voice and this time he realized that they were both female.

If they are not Wehrmacht, they must be collaborators? Those are even more dangerous. "I am inspecting the railway," Claude lied. It was an absurd response, but he was still quite shaken from having been caught unaware. He took a moment to beat himself up, as was his custom.

There were some murmurs and then a voice replied, "We're running out of time. Just...see that he doesn't move."

Then Claude noticed one of the shadows brush by him. *Is that a nun carrying a landmine?* He wondered. *Maybe I set off the grenades and spilled my brains on the trestle?* Then, a couple more of the sisters walked past him. *Wait! No, I'm dead! That's why...nuns!*

"I have no idea where we should put this--" concluded Sister Marie, who swung the mine about recklessly; by its handle.

"On the track," replied Sister Gabrielle. She jumped back to avoid being hit.

"It'll just push it aside," complained Sister Beatrice. "It has to be at the same level."

"I don't know why we thought we could do this," sighed Sister Marie. "We're experts at Sacrament...not sabotage!"

Claude, who had been caught in a most uncomfortable position between squatting and standing, felt reassured enough to rise completely; at which point he heard a most unsettling stretching sound. It caused him to freeze though he could not quite place it. "Look at my feet. See those explosives? I received a communique with the rail info. That's why I'm here. I might be able to help you?"

"Yes, you're clearly a pro," mocked Sister Dominique, taking note of the string in his hand.

Sister Marie signaled her approval and Claude felt himself lifted to his feet and pushed forward. He turned around to find Sister Dominique, who addressed the business end of an arrow at him.

"I don't know what's more unsettling, the nun with the landmine...or the one with the bow?" He walked over to Sister Marie and Gabrielle, who had laid the anti-tank mine half-way on the track. "That will not work at all. Anyway, the train is never going to make it this far as I have already rigged an explosive thirty meters back."

"Are you going to help or not," replied Sister Marie.

Claude smiled, "Your disguises are so authentic. I wish I had thought of that." He placed the mine upon some rocks so that it would sit even with the track and then rigged a knife, upon the trigger. He worked for another minute and announced, "That just might do it, and the train should almost be here. We must leave at once!"

They ran to the west side of the trestle, where Claude stood with his twine, ready to activate his trap. Soon, they heard the singing of the rails, in the distance. As the train approached, Claude yanked on his cord. He had not, however, taken into account that being askew the trestle, would change the angle from which he pulled. Nothing happened. He tugged furiously, but the train was now almost upon it. Claude took both hands and gave one strong pull, but being entangled with one of the ties; it simply ripped free. The twine became limp in his hands as the train rolled past his trap.

Then, there was a great explosion as its wheels ran over the nun's anti-tank mine. The running gear of the locomotive was thrown vertical, and its axle box flew apart. The train lifted off the rails and became, entirely, dislodged. Next, the engine rolled off the trestle and plummeted into the ravine, which dragged three of the other cars with it. Within this chain of events, the safety of one of Claude's grenades, somehow, became dislodged. They exploded under the very freight car that carried the armaments shipment. The series of explosions were like great cymbals wielded by the Giant of Castelnau and proved so severe that they nearly vaporized the cars that remained.

The nuns lay flat on the wet grass and clutched their ears, as pieces of debris whistled by overhead. A piece of rail imbedded in a chêne verte tree behind them. They were not prepared for the flashes of light, from the explosions, so they became feckless and narrow. Unable to see the effects of their sabotage, they waited for the whirlwind of dust to dissipate.

When the blasts were, but intermittent, Claude looked at the nuns and scoffed, "Beginners luck!"

Sister Marie turned and asked bluntly, "Who are you?"

"I am Claude Delacroix of the Maquis de Vabre. Vive la resistance!"

CHAPTER EIGHT
THE LABYRINTH WE MAKE

Sister Marie looked at Claude, like a pardon that had arrived after the blade had fallen. Her veil was covered with the ash that fell in flurries of gray snowflakes. "Monsieur Delacroix, you're not an easy man to find."

"That is good to hear. I am not exactly running for office. I am running, but usually...away." He wiped the dust from his eyes and pulled down his beret. Isolation had coarsened his social skills and made him ill at ease around others.

"You are a maquisard? How many of you are there?" asked Sister Beatrice. She viewed every day as an opportunity to grow her knowledge.

"Counting me...one. Well, there are others, but we are spread quite thin; which is why I was sent here. We have answered the call of de Gaulle to embrace the path of resistance. It's not easy to hide and network. It's like trying to throw a party without sending out invitations." He realized that he had questions of his own. "So, you are really nuns? No?"

"Oui and perhaps, we can be of help?" offered Marie. "We have many unique skills."

Claude smiled, "Well, I welcome your prayers, but such as tonight...I cannot allow it. It'd be like inviting a mortician to a christening."

"Is that a no?" Sister Gabrielle asked, astonished.

"Of course, I am saying no. What do you think? I can not have the blood of nuns on my hands. My dearly departed mother would kill me. She would come back to life and accomplish that which the Germans have not been able. Anyway, it has been lovely meeting you, but prends soin de toi."

The nuns just stood in place, staring at him.

"Au revoir," Claude continued, but still they didn't move. So...adieu? Bonne soirée. Kick rocks. You know...get thee to a nunnery?"

Immediately, Sister Dominique drew her bow and released a bolt right at Claude's head. It grazed his sideburn and pierced the eye socket of a German soldier, who had snuck up on him; pistol drawn.

Claude watched the Nazi tumble back down the ravine where he created a small plumb of smoke. He tilted his head as if searching for further objections, then replied, "Well...perhaps a trial period, might not be without some justification?"

Klaus looked at his putrid-green Kübelwagen and rolled his eyes. "Friedrich. Where is the morning train? There is something very special I am waiting for."

"Really?" Friedrich replied, astonished. "What can it be?" It was not like his commander to be expectant of anything.

Klaus tilted his black cap as if he was the Nazi Maurice Chevalier. "Well, I didn't want to say anything, but you know that Daimler-Benz G4 I've wanted?"

"No--" Friedrich replied astonished. It was almost like he was the one receiving the car. After all, most of the time, he would be its driver. Their standing among the other officers would rise, exponentially, as they arrived in the 3,700 kilogram behemoth; command flags waving from its fenders. Who cared if it was useless off-road, when everywhere they went they would create their own parade.

"Yes, I pulled a few strings, well tugged is more like it, and it is being delivered this very morning. The person it was intended for was assassinated!"

"That's marvelous!" remarked Friedrich.

"Isn't it?" laughed Klaus. He noticed that Friedrich gave him a knowing, but approving eye. "No, Friedrich, it wasn't me...not that I wouldn't. I mean, wait 'till you see this thing! I'd put a bullet in you."

Friedrich was about to start the car when he noticed a Gerfreiter running up to them frantically. They waved their arms and handed Klaus a letter. "Herr Metzger, the train never arrived with the munitions. It was sabotaged as it traveled over a high trestle."

"This is terrible news," replied Friedrich.

"It is beyond terrible! My new car was on that train!" Klaus pounded his fists, repeatedly, on the dash of the Kübelwagen, until the whole thing shook like a rowboat that might capsize.

René had never noticed how delicate Chloé's wrists were, or how graceful the nape of her neck. As she lay out a flannel blanket and arranged the accessories for their picnic, he thought, *French woman truly are the most beautiful in the world.* He had only been to England, once, but his opinion remained unchanged. Perhaps the ugliness of war amplified the virtue of what few shards of beauty remained.

"Voilà!" she announced. "Everything is ready. I picked the strawberries this morning. You can dip it in this crème--"

"Is that quiche?" René asked. It had been so long since he had seen the dish, that he waited for confirmation before allowing his hopes to be raised.

"Oui, with bacon and leek." She pretended not to anticipate the reaction such a statement would assure.

René nearly fainted from delight. "Truly, this is the greatest day of my life." It was the happiest he had been since he had fled Paris.

"René, this place is lovely, but won't it be a problem that no one can reach you?"

"Quelle horreur!" René teased. "When you are the mayor of Brassac, it is best that no one can reach you." He took a bite of the quiche and his eyes rolled back in his head.

Chloé noticed the unusual label on the wine that he had brought. "Is this wine German?"

"It's a long story," he replied, chagrinned. "It grates a bit on the palette, but it's free and plentiful."

She poured herself a glass and winced as she took a sip. "Lovely," she lied. She could tell that René had, already, completely succumbed to her charms. He, enthusiastically, helped himself to the baguette and a small disk of Reblochon that she had brought. "There is something I've wanted to ask you."

"Anything," he replied, his mouth full of coulommiers.

"Noele was my best friend. Does it bother you?"

René shrugged. "Not at all. Vous?"

She did not want to appear cold or to lack loyalty. "I'm not sure how to feel. She did decide to become a nun, so there is definitely no future for the two of you."

He was unsure if she was truly inquisitive or if this was her attempt, psychologically, to clear the room of any lingering hope he might have for her. "I still care about her deeply, but Noele has chosen her path and I support her completely."

"Do you feel guilt?" Chloé was familiar with the story of how he had fled Brassac, the night before they were to be wed. There was not a man, woman, or child who was not aware of the drama that ensued from that fateful decision.

"I wasn't ready to get married. I felt trapped, so I ran. Do I regret the way I did it? Of course, but it would have been worse had I gone through with it. I should have been honest with her sooner, but I was a coward."

It was the opportunity for which Chloé had waited. "You need not worry about me pushing marriage. I don't even believe there is a future."

"I certainly hope not," René replied, as they began to kiss.

"Philippe, I know you are home!" yelled Sister Marie, picking up a bottle she found in his front yard.

On the other side of his pea green door, Philippe cringed. "Damn nuns," he cried. "Why can't they just leave me alone?" *Crash.* He opened the door to find that wine dripped from the frame and threshold. "What do you think you're doing?"

Sister Marie bumped his shoulder as she let herself in.

"Knocking didn't seem to get me anywhere." She considered Philippe's mess of a living room as if conducting a forensic examination of his soul. "It looks like the sequel to Verdun was fought in here. Where's Madame Adéle?"

Philippe did not bother to respond, but went around the room and made a half-hearted attempt at tidying. It was not so much that he cared about appearances, but he did not want to give the nun the satisfaction of being right.

"She left you, did she? Was it the drinking?" Sister Marie tried to count the stacks of bottles strewn about the room, but finally admitted defeat. She waited while Philippe cleared her off a place to sit.

"She has gone to her mother's house in Mazamet...not that I care." Philippe lit himself a cigarette, which quickly filled the room with a putrid, blue smoke.

Sister Marie did not buy his attempt at indifference. It was the same way, he brushed off rejection, as a boy, when the other children hurt him at school. "What happened to you, Philippe? Is it that you don't care, or that you need to be numb for the road you travel?" The time had come to touch upon the real reason for her visit. "You've been spending quite a bit of time with the Germans. Haven't you?"

"And so what if I have? It is only sensible. We're occupied by them, aren't we?" He wondered how much she knew about his involvement with their latest residents. He knew she wouldn't approve of his decision to join the Service d'ordre légionnaire.

"When everything is falling apart, it can be very tempting to grab the first thing that appears to be a rope, but be careful that it's not a snake." She knew that Philippe had already chosen his destination, but she would illuminate the path of escape; should he ever desire to take it.

"The British are bombing French civilians," he replied and took a long drag. It was true that occupied France had many ports and military targets that had drawn Allied attention. A great number of woman and children had been killed in the attacks.

"You're just mimicking propaganda." Sister Marie had seen the posters, but knew that facts were nothing, but the bastard child of truth, when separated from their context. "Can't you see what they do Philippe? They give you just enough to make the lies go down. She got up and kicked the dust off her feet. "Well...I can see now that I've failed you."

"Sister, if the Germans won't protect us from the British, who will? Only they can keep us fed."

"Philippe, I know the difference between compassion and well-calculated tyranny. Do you?" She showed herself out the door and did not bother to say, "Adieu."

For his part, he decided the best response was to open a vintage bottle of Beaujolais, but her words burned like acid in the back of his throat. Philippe threw the bottle back until it exceeded his ability to swallow, and he choked like a drowning man.

Klaus caught himself in time to avoid falling down the ravine. Pieces of the train were strewn about, in fragments too small to be identified. His foot hooked onto one of the rail wheels, which brought him to a sudden stop. "General Eckart will definitely take notice of this," he mumbled. A request for additional munitions, of such quantity, would not go unnoticed. Especially, when they were dearly needed for areas where an Allied invasion was a pressing threat. *What if the request is denied?* He looked around to see if anything could be salvaged, but all around him, steel and iron were tangled up like the knotted chain of a necklace. Now his thoughts returned to Pabianice, where he had found himself in a similar predicament, ill-equipped with a determined enemy. *They blamed me because they couldn't accept that they had failed to plan. The last time they transferred me. Who knows what will happen if I fail again?* "Friedrich, why do we not yet have the names for the local resistance?"

Friedrich, however, was occupied by a gruesome sight. "This soldier. He has been shot with an arrow." Then he noticed something glimmer underneath the mud. "Oh, and I found a piece of your car!"

"Any idea how I knew about the train?" Claude waited for a response, from the nuns, to see if they were paying attention. "A Jewish friend of mine, is in charge of the railways in Tarn. The resistance is everywhere and nowhere. We must be like vapor, but materialize in an instant, if necessary. Information is the lifeblood of the resistance, but so is secrecy. Now usually, we meet with no more than two other members, that is in case we are infiltrated, but I see this will have to be an exception. This will be considered one operational group--"

"What are we called?" asked Sister Gabrielle.

"You're not called anything," Claude replied.

"Well, we have to be called something," protested Sister Beatrice.

"I've got it!" cried Sister Dominique. "How about, The Nazi Killing Nun Club?"

"Sister! That's too violent," Anette admonished her. "It has to be something tasteful that reflects our calling. I suggest Nuns Who Love Guns. See..it has 'love' in the title."

"The whole point is to keep people from knowing you're a part of the resistance...like my friend. There will be no name." Claude was starting to understand that his work was cut out for him.

"Even weapons are collected after every mission. That way if you are searched, you will be found innocent."

"That's no problem, Father Jubé can hold them for us and we have prepared other means of protecting ourselves." Marie pulled out a leather strap, with bullet casings sewn upon it. It looked like an implement that might have been handed down by her medieval predecessors. It was unusual, but not entirely out of character for a nun whose normality had always been in doubt.

"And what exactly do you call that?" Claude was curious though not entirely sure he wanted to know.

"Corporal Punishment," she replied, and brought it down on a melon. As it shattered, it splashed juice upon his face.

Sister Dominique stepped forward and held out her bow. "I call this St. Sebastian's Revenge."

Claude wiped melon from his eye, with his handkerchief. "Yes, we've already been introduced, but I don't think a saint would want revenge."

Sister Dominique threw her bow over his head and snapped the string against his Adam's apple. "I'm the nun!"

The maquisard cried out in agony. His neck had a red line that he would carry for the next several days.

Dominique noticed Sister Marie's disapproval. "Ok, I see your point. Just St. Sebastian."

Claude wondered if it might not have been better to have been captured by the Germans at the trestle. The nuns seemed to share their capacity for being efficiently sadistic. "Well, we have not received any airdrops from the British SOE, so we must make due with what we have. The Nazis are also, now, lacking thanks to our efforts. We are called the Maquis because we hide amid the brush. The night is ours, but we are not of the night. Liberty. Equality. Fraternity. These ideas cannot be erased, as long as we resist."

Sister Marie looked at her sisters who had supported her, when she only had the strength to fall. They were her dearest and most loyal friends; a family not of blood, but of the soul. She knew that she spoke for each and every one of them when she replied, "Monsieur Claude...resistance is what we live for."

CHAPTER NINE
A PILOT WORTH SAVING

Through cracked, leather-framed goggles, the RAF pilot tried to will his fuel gauges to reflect anything other than his own, dire observations. He flicked them, just to be sure, but while the Spitfire Mk IX's supercharged Merlin 61 engine continued its distinctive growl, the needles refused to lie, or provide him with undue comfort. The vibrations from its valves and cylinders, still spoke to him through his seat and rudder pedals, but there was no denying the approach of the inevitable. *How'd I let that Jerry separate me from the* group, he wondered. *I'm an old lag, dammit!"* There was a fine line between retreat and cowardice, but though he continued to second-guess himself, the situation had become entirely cocked up. His only regret was not retreating from that Focke-Wulf 190, in a more sensible direction, and anywhere, but east. If his Spitfire's elliptical wings hadn't been able to out turn them, he would have been singing with the angels. He wondered if he would have even been able to escape in his old plane, the one that had shepherded him through The Battle of Britain. Still, the newer Mk IX's Type C wing had delivered him from the gates of Perdition although eventual entry seemed all, but certain. It seemed a blasted waste to scuttle a perfectly good bird, and he was brassed off about it. He had grown attached to the airplane and felt cornered into putting an old friend down.

He descended to a more reasonable altitude and threw off his mask, whose rubber seal chaffed against his face. It was evident he should have waited a few thousand more feet, as his chart seemed out of focus for a few seconds. Until now, he had only thought of his aircraft, but the time had arrived to consider skin that wasn't aluminum. Every option placed him in occupied territory, with only a remote chance that the French Resistance might find him. Like a prisoner forced to select his preferred form of execution, he weighed the pros and cons of the various French towns and forests upon which he might impale himself. Then his finger noticed Toulouse. It was further still to the east, but it was also the area from which the Luftwaffe operated the Dornier Do 217s, the German Luftwaffe's flying pencil bomber. They had been making quite a mess of the shipping channels in the Mediterranean and giving the navy ample misery. It seemed like a solid way to go out a hero and not a half-pint one at that. At any rate, it was unlikely that he would get out alive; even if he did manage to survive the jump. Still, was it better to be shot by the side of the road, tangled in a parachute like a trapped animal, or like a real knight of the air; sacrificing oneself for king and country?

The Spitfire could not realize that its mortality had been determined. Metal and flesh had knit together to achieve singularity within the womb of the sky. In return for the gift of flight, he had imbued it with his soul and now its destruction would forfeit a piece of himself. Though he had never ridden a horse, he imagined that the melding of animus was correlative. He knew he would have to fulfill its trust by doing his part to help it live out its complete and created purpose.

Apparently, the Germans understood the value of Toulouse because he had barely reached Moissac when two ME109s descended, upon him, their cannons blazing. The red and orange flashes of light would have been beautiful if they were not blossoms of death, which grew exclusively in the season of war.

Like sloths, the nuns shimmied along the rope that Claude had secured between the two holm oak trees. Their rosary beads dangled from about their necks as they hung, a nun and a half above the ground. Sister Marie, who had already made it to the platform on the other side, encouraged the others and wondered if the line could hold their combined weight.

"Seriously? I have trained grandmothers who moved faster," Claude mocked. "Dead grandmothers." He leaned against the tree, but did not at all like the way the moss felt against his hand and wiped his pants, which left a green stain.

Sister Dominique was too frustrated to put up with the morose Frenchman. "Keep it up Claude, and when I get down from here, I'm going to hit you with my ruler, so hard, you'll speak Chinese."

This seemed to give him some reservations about his approach to training. "I have no idea what that means...but you can save it for the Germans."

"Can somebody please move," cried Sister Noele, "I'm getting tired, and I'm going to fall."

Sister Dominique's face was flushed. "I'd like to, but Anette won't move!"

"I'm going as fast as I--" Suddenly, Sister Anette slipped, and her hands fell off the rope. Her legs held, but she swung backwards and grabbed onto Dominique's habit.

"Get off me! Let go, or I'm going to fall." She fought against Anette. "Just drop!" Her legs slipped, and the rope dug into her fingers as she tried to hold on.

"I'm scared! I don't want to fall!" Anette wrapped her calves around Sister Dominique, who was only able to support their combined weight, briefly. They crashed onto the leafy floor of the forest; entwined in a pile.

"I'm falling too," cried Sister Noele, who could no longer wait out the pile-up. "Look out below!" She fell onto them as Robespierre jumped upon the stack and yelped in excitement.

Claude rolled his eyes at Sister Marie nonplussed who replied,

"You should see how they started out as nuns."

Next, Claude led them on a ten kilometer hike through the hills of the Sidobre region. He taught them to use ropes, handholds, and how to balance themselves on the granite rocks. He demonstrated the method to pinch a positive outside edge and then to use pockets, within the limestone, to pull themselves up. "The Germans are conditioned for war from the time they are children. Membership in the Hitlerjugend is a requirement for them. We...know how to identify cheese."

"And I've been doling out punishment since I entered the convent," Sister Dominique protested.

"The Hitler Youth teaches them how to follow orders. It provides them with rigorous physical conditioning, how to work as a team, weapons training--" Claude looked at the nuns who struggled to make it to the fifth kilometer marker and wondered if he had made a mistake. They seemed grossly out of shape.

"How much further?" Gabrielle panted. "I think I just pulled my appendix."

"It's not your physical endurance I'm testing," Claude remarked. "I don't fear Nazis because of their muscles."

At about the ninth kilometer Sister Gabrielle, whose legs were shorter by half, than most, fell to her knees and lay on the ground gasping.

123

Sister Marie ran over to help, but Gabrielle motioned her away. "No one help me," she replied. "I can do this. I don't need help."

Sister Dominique would have none of it though. She put her arm around her neck and lifted her from the ground. "Don't you fight me, Gabrielle. I'm going to carry you. Not because you're weak...God help anyone who calls you weak, but because you're my sister."

"Good," observed Claude. "That is the teamwork I saw at the trestle. Maybe I wasn't wrong, but you have much to learn. Next we train with weapons, and I think it's time I met Father Jubé...formally."

The afternoon clouds flashed, angrily, above the safe house in Moissac, where Michel and Jacob had determined to wait out the war. It brought to mind Zeus attacking Salmoneus, except that occasionally a silver or blue wing would break through the vaporous shroud of the firmament. Michel ran outside to discover that, incredibly, it was a lone British Spitfire pilot that had engaged the two German Messerschmitts. Able to assume the outcome, he almost went back inside to make lunch, but Jacob appeared at the door and tried to run past him. Michel made a gate of his arms and attempted to placate him. "Stay inside for now and I'll see if it's okay."

The birds of prey flew tight, concentric, circles as they fought to get inside their enemy's six o'clock. Unlike the engagement with the Focke-Wulf 190 that had started his day, the lead Messerschmitt pilot seemed more than willing to bank his plane until the wings snapped. Then, the Luftwaffe fired his cannons, and the vibration caused his wings to pitch, ever so slightly, enough that his left wing exceeded its angle of attack and dropped. He rolled the plane over on its back, but he was, temporarily, removed from the chase. His wingman was still on the Spitfire's tail, but maybe this Messerschmitt pilot was too careful. With a fearlessness that arose from having assumed himself already dead the RAF pilot yanked on his stick until he thought, it might break off. His left wing was practically pointed at the ground as his sights covered the ME109. The first burst from his 20mm Hispano Mk II cannons struck the bullet-proof plate behind the ME109 pilot, but the second hit the fuel tanks and the explosion ripped the plane apart. A black cloud entered the heavens, as did another soul.

There was no time to celebrate. The red fuel light on his panel reminded him that his juice was nearly depleted. His Spitfire was flying on nothing, but determination and British resolve. The lead Messerschmitt had recovered to see their friend, fall to the ground in pieces. The rage-fueled dive that followed was a banshee-like cry for revenge. The RAF pilot hauled back on his stick and pointed the nose of his plane towards Polaris. The ME109 pilot matched his climb and shot skyward like a V1 rocket hell-bent on terrorizing London.

Now he wished that the Spitfire didn't have such good rear visibility because he could look back and see the ME109's 20mm propeller hub cannon, pursue him like an angry hornet. The German pilot let his cannons loose and tore off the tip of his tail.

The Spitfire had no intention of letting him have another bite. He slammed his stick against his knee and stomped full, bottom rudder. The ME109 whizzed by him, but now he fell out of control for three thousand feet. When he had recovered, he spied the German above him at his two o'clock. His fuel light pleaded, but if he bailed out too low, he'd be an anchor. Climbing to engage, might mean running out of gas and becoming an easy mark.

The Luftwaffe pilot could hardly believe that the Brit would volunteer himself for such a disadvantages position. He smiled, pointed his ME109 towards the earth, and dove; cannons blazing. To his surprise, however, as they rushed to join wings, he struggled to keep sight of his advisory against the patchwork of French farmlands and forests. The Spitfire's guns remained silent, and stealth became its advantage. Now it was, but a test to see who would be first to loose his wool and stray from the centerline. The luxury of having more options now became the German's undoing, as he blinked and banked hard. The Spitfire remained hidden no more as it materialized, in time, to fill the ME109's wings with a constellation of stars.

Then, everything grew quiet as the Merlin 61 drank its last drop of life, sputtered, and died. The propeller froze, and the Spitfire hung in the air, like a diver at the moment their vertical momentum expired. The Spitfire fell back on its tail, and the RAF pilot pushed forward on his stick to stabilize what was now a glider. Nothing more could be asked from his plane, which felt as if its spirit had departed, leaving only a frame. Its pilot also had nothing left to give, so he lifted his seat and slid back the canopy. He unlatched the cockpit door and reached behind his seat to grab the one item that he truly treasured, his logbook. Written in various scripts, and colors of ink, was the record of all of his flights and endorsements from the hands of the only people he had ever respected, many no longer alive. He gripped his parachute's ripcord as he allowed himself to step outside the plane and into the slipstream. The Spitfire provided one final service by not striking him with its tail, as he tumbled past it. The plane was not done fighting, however, as it rammed into a house where German officers were quartered and set it ablaze. As he dangled in the sky, he saw the second Messerschmitt impact the ground and produce a ball of fire that reminded him of the cauliflower; he missed back in

Devonshire. It was quite likely that he would never taste it again, but he was satisfied with his time.

From the ground, Michel watched these events unfold, astonished. *There*, he thought, *was a pilot worth saving,* and he ran towards him to do just that.

Father Jubé ushered Sister Marie and the sullen-eyed Frenchman who accompanied her, into his office. She loved the way it smelled inside, a mixture of old books and candle wax. "Do you know who this is?" she asked, closing the door behind them and drawing the shades.

Father Jubé was too busy for games. "Charles de Gaulle? Marie, if you want to give someone shelter you don't have to involve me."

She grabbed a doily and held it over his face.

"Claude Delacroix!" Father Jubé cried astonished. He rose to shake the Frenchman's hand. "I couldn't make you out without the screen. Where ever did you find him?"

"Apparently, we both have an interest in trains," Marie replied.

"Oui," said Claude, in his flat Gallic accent. "I was not sure if you were part of the resistance or I would have made myself more available."

"Did you go and sin no more?" asked Father Jubé, playfully.

"I don't know," replied Claude, pithily. "Did you keep my confession confidential?"

"Touché, but I don't think you would have given me your name if you weren't trying to determine whether or not you had any friends in the area."

Claude was impressed by the priest's keen awareness of his situation. "I have received considerable support from local clergy, so yes...it was something of a test." He removed his beret. "One cannot go long, in these parts, without hearing about Father Jubé. I did not see how I could avoid such a man...for long."

Father Jubé was never sure how to respond to such compliments, but they always had the effect of restoring the awkwardness that he had tried to leave behind with his youth. "I'm sure they were mistakingly projecting qualities, from the one I serve. Won't you have a seat?"

"I understand you supplied the tank mine?" Claude continued.

"Yes, a gift from one of my parishioners. I asked for candles, but you find the most curious things in the donation box."

Sister Marie put her lips close to his ear. "He was interested in seeing what other assets we might have. He, also, needs a safe place of storage."

"How do I know you're not a German?" asked Father Jubé. "I

have a friend in Montauban who was arrested and his seminary closed--"

"I guess you will have to have faith," Claude replied, a stock answer he had used with priests on more than one occasion.

Father Jubé, was aware of his little ploy, so he looked to Marie. He trusted her judgment, more than his own, and his instincts told him to be wary.

"It's okay Francis."

He contemplated Claude, who seemed more sinner than saint. His eyes had the weariness he had seen in soldiers whom he had known on the front. "Well, I suppose if Marie says you are okay, I will have to trust you, but then she has always given me far too much credit. Still, she is a better judge of character, than I."

"Now, remember...I never said I had good character," Claude laughed, taking out a cigarette.

"Please don't smoke in my office," Father Jubé requested, as he slid back the bookcase. "You might blow yourself up." He opened the door to reveal the rifles, grenades, and ammunition they had been able to compile. "Here is everything we've gathered, thus far. I hope that it might be of some use to you in your work."

"Thank you," replied Sister Marie grabbing a gun and several boxes of bullets. "I know it will."

Father Jubé looked at her flummoxed, wondering if he had missed something in the conversation. She hid things under her habit as fast as her hands would allow.

"She didn't tell you?" Claude marveled. "I'm training her and the other sisters."

The ground rushed to greet the falling RAF pilot and much faster than he had expected. He hit the dirt hard. After so many hours in the cockpit, his legs were not adequately prepared to support such a sudden impact of his weight. He gathered up his parachute and pulled his pistol; which he liked to call his barker.

Michel breached the clearing to find the nervous pilot addressing it at him. Fortunately, his manner of dress and expression of alarm made it clear that he was not a man of arms. The pilot smiled, chagrined, and waved to indicate that he no longer saw him as a threat.

Then a German personnel vehicle, with four soldiers, barreled into the field. They had followed the pilot's descent in the hope of intercepting him. The pilot pointed his pistol at the car's front window and fired several shots. Its driver slumped over the steering wheel, but the car kept rolling and slammed into him.

Michel darted behind a grainstack, as the sound of additional shots filled the clearing. Not interested in having to answer any questions, however, he left uncertain of the outcome. He did not stop until he had reached the house where Jacob still waited. "It's not safe."

"Is he dead?" asked Klaus, looking up from a mountain of documents. He was so understaffed that he found himself fighting paperwork, as much as the war itself. His office was in the former residence of a wealthy factory owner. The French manor-house was an elegant way to pass the many monotonous hours as he awaited combat's punctuation. Klaus did not sleep in the family's former private chambers, located on the first floor. It seemed, entirely, too susceptible to a coups de main.

"No," replied Friedrich. "He was shot twice, in the shoulder and then hit by a car. They took him to a local hospital. He is in stable condition and can soon be transferred."

"I see." Klaus looked at an expense report and wondered who he hated more, the British or his accountants. "What kind of plane was he flying?"

"A Spitfire." Friedrich was accustomed to only half of Klaus' attention, at any time. "He shot down two other planes before crashing."

"Well, why are they bothering me? It's not even the right type of plane to drop supplies. Hardly what they use to transfer messages to the resistance. He must have been lost."

"They thought he might have information that would help us?"

"Highly unlikely. He was flying a fighter. I'm sure he had no intention of finding himself near our jurisdiction. Tell them to transfer him to a dugaluft and be done with it."

"Yes sir."

He looked outside and saw a couple soldiers fashioning fishing poles. "Wait...on second thought, Friedrich, do you like to fish?"

"Nein." He was not sure why Klaus would ask him such a random question.

"Of course not. Fishing takes patience. You have to lure the fish into taking the bait." He put down his pen and covered his upper lip, with his index finger, to focus his thoughts. "I wonder if this pilot might not be a way to flush out the local resistance? Transferring pilots, back to their bases, is one of their primary concerns. Is it not?"

Friedrich smiled and was a bit disappointed that he had not thought of the notion. "Yes, he might be useful as bait. He might be very useful."

"I don't want him in a luftstalag until the resistance comes around sniffing. However, I don't think Toulouse is a tempting enough hook. The best type of trap is close and familiar. Now if you'll excuse me...I'm going fishing."

CHAPTER TEN
A VERY GOOD THIEF

Léon patted his jacket, and the blood drained from his bug-eyed, gaunt expression. *My wallet's gone!* He frantically looked left and right. Around him, every face was known, and why wouldn't they be? In such a town, every citizen was identified by their capacity. He was the local thief, which was a pitiable role, but one he owned; nonetheless. His Adam's apple searched to-and-fro until it pointed towards a gaunt-looking man who nervously exited from a nearby doorway. Léon ran up to him and put his hand on his shoulder. "Hello friend, I don't think I know you?"

"Sorry, I'm in a bit of a hurry."

"Oh, that's no problem, but I think I'll need my wallet before you go."

The man's eyes darted, skittishly. "I have no idea what you're talking about."

Léon grabbed his jacket and leaned in close. "I know you are not from here, but...it is simply not possible to steal anything from me."

"Like I said, I don't know what you're talking about. If you will excuse me?"

Léon puffed out his bottom lip and shrugged. "Maybe, you're right? I seem to have found it, just now." He tauntingly waved his wallet back at the man.

The man patted himself down and realized that Léon had been able to snatch it back from him. "I'm glad you were able to find it," he covered.

"Yes," replied Léon, cooly. "Such an unfortunate misunderstanding, but it would be best that you do not come back to Brassac. It's not safe here, for you."

The young man looked down, defeated, and shuffled away.

"Aren't you forgetting something," asked Father Jubé, who startled Léon from behind.

Léon gulped, disappointed to have been taken by surprise twice in one morning. "I hate when you do that! Fine!" He produced a watch he had, also, lifted from the thief and threw it with all his might. The man, who was now twenty meters away, jerked as it nailed the back of his head. "It wasn't a very good watch, anyway. He did have it coming though, didn't he? Like the Germans?"

"It's not about who has it coming. Léon...haven't I taught you anything?"

The thief searched his memory, but he could not understand Father Jubé's correction. He had received the priest's loving chastisements for so long, that he had come to recognize their value. It was, in fact, a validation of his character, that he did not resent the priest's rebukes or seek out less-judgmental company; as weaker souls might. Léon was not so haughty that he became defensive. He would have been astonished if he knew that it was, for that fact alone, that Father Jubé felt he had more potential than any of his other parishioners.

"Are the supplies ready for the sisters?" the priest asked.

"Yes, well-hidden under the hay. Such a cart, driven by a priest should provide no difficulties."

Father Jubé had more in mind than recompense for Léon, and he now felt he had found the opportunity to see his plan through. "Bien. They are waiting for us at a secret location in the forest."

"Why do I have to go? They make me uncomfortable."

"They're nuns...that's their job, and I want you to see that for which you work. A farmer needs to see his seeds become crops if he is to be motivated to plant for the coming year." He stuck out his hand for Léon, who he pulled up beside him on the horse-drawn cart. Father Jubé nudged the horses, and they bounced over the cobblestones, towards their camp, hidden in the Sidobre.

Klaus threw down the envelope. "General Eckart is coming next week!" The vein on his forehead did not escape Friedrich's notice. He felt his stress as it trickled down to him. "He would not visit if he thought things were in order. There have been too many small incidents, including the loss of munitions. It would be most beneficial to tell him that we had captured one of the resistance leaders."

Friedrich placed his dagger against his cheek so that he could enjoy its cool steel. Klaus' office was usually too warm for his liking, and the blade was a sort of refreshment for him. He never stopped to reflect on how many people's interiors it had pierced. "As you instructed, I have made the arrangements to transport the RAF pilot to a more local hospital. It should prove most tempting to the type of fish we are trying to catch." He stopped to determine if Klaus was paying attention or too absorbed in the thought of the General's visit, to appreciate his planning. "Naturally, it will be filled with SS personnel dressed as hospital employees. The people assigned, directly, to him will all be Gestapo. His wounds are no longer sufficient to not have been transferred; so we will forbid any contact with the civilian staff. We will, however, ensure that everyone knows that he is there."

Klaus nodded approvingly, and forced himself to focus on the matter at hand. "You know, I'd like to use this opportunity to test our mayor in Brassac. I'm not sure how yet, but he seems too indifferent to our presence."

"Isn't that good?" Friedrich was always trying to learn from his master. He marveled at how he could wield the weapon of bureaucracy, the way he might a knife.

"We have invaded his home and he should be agitated. The fact that he is not, tells me he is not being entirely honest. I would feel more assured if it were, ever so slightly, apparent that he did not like me, but was willing to acquiesce. To be so agreeable, is clearly an indication of deceit."

It was at moments like this that Friedrich understood why Klaus was the one who sat behind the desk. He looked at his dagger and wondered if his inability to see into the hearts of men, was why his role was limited to expressions of physical will. The only time he ever worried was when he considered what might happen to him if he was someday denied access to Klaus' insight. Then he would be, but a blunt tool; and an easily discarded one. "You could tell him about the pilot--"

"I plan to, but everyone will know about that. That's the whole point. I'm not sure yet, but it will come to me."

At the camp, Sister Gabrielle groaned as she pushed herself up from the wet, leaf and pine-covered, floor of the forest. She was not used to strength-training exercises, and she was beet red as she struggled to lift herself; again and again.

"I think that's enough for one day," offered Sister Marie.

Gabrielle did not agree with her conclusion though she

appeared as if she might pass out. "I won't be the weak link. I'm going to be the strongest nun in all of France!"

Marie knelt beside her. "There are different ways to measure strength. The links of our chain are different and isn't that good? Look at Sister Anette. She fell from the rope, and no one faults her. Can you imagine a chain of nothing, but Sister Dominiques?"

Dominique, who stood nearby, shrugged as if she did not see that as a bad proposition, at all.

Gabrielle groaned and tried to do another pushup. "You always say those kinds of things."

Sister Marie implored Sister Dominique, with a look whose purpose was to compel her to say something. "Encourage her!" she whispered, between her teeth.

Sister Dominique furrowed her brow as if she tried to search for the right words, but finally shouted, "Robespierre...a hand."

The dog jumped up on Gabrielle's back, and his additional weight caused her to fall flat on her face.

"I meant a word of encouragement," clarified Marie, pushing her forward.

Dominique looked down at Sister Gabrielle and said, "You're not that weak...just small--"

"Please gather around, sisters," interrupted Claude. "I'm going to teach you how to escape handcuffs." He put them on to demonstrate, but quickly realized that he couldn't get out. "I'm a little embarrassed. Does anyone have a saw?" Eventually, he remembered the correct technique and was able to free himself. The sisters took turns escaping with various degrees of success. "These are your cyanide pills. They are standard issue--"

"We won't need them, thank you," Sister Marie informed him.

"If someone catches you it would be very bad," Claude protested.

"It is against our beliefs." She was appalled by the notion.

"And killing Nazis isn't?"

"We're still working on that one," replied Beatrice.

"I'm not," said Dominique.

"Fine, don't get caught. Let's move on to this chart that explains how to recognize German rank, and we'll briefly discuss the organization of the Gestapo," but then he hushed at the sound of wheels rolling over gravel. Everyone was relieved to see Father Jubé and Léon arrive, with their supplies.

"Do you think I'm losing my edge?" Léon had not stopped grousing about having his wallet stolen, the whole way to the nun's training camp.

"No, Léon," Father Jubé reassured him. "You are a very good thief."

"I know, right?" His eyes hung low upon his face. "Nobody steals from me!"

Father Jubé smiled, "You should worry about the things we all give away willingly, but that matter most of all."

"I was just explaining the Gestapo," said Claude, who welcomed them to their little camp. "Your mayor is often seen in their company,"

"Well, that is his job," the priest, reflected, as he tied up their mule. "Sometimes, it's best to keep your enemies close. The real question is what to do with them, when given the opportunity."

Sister Marie allowed Father Jubé to come to his former student's defense, but felt responsible for putting René in such a position, in the first place. She knew that someone had to represent the interests of the town, and it was her way of moving his issues, with Noele, back into play. Confronting issues head-on had always been her style.

"Is the mayor of Brassac someone who can be trusted?" asked Claude.

Noele noticed that everyone's eyes focused on her. She reflected for a moment, then replied honestly, "He is a flawed, but good man."

"Are you familiar with him?"

She smiled, but looked away. "He's my ex-fiancée."

Claude was bemused. "And I thought I was complicated. Well," he asked Father Jubé, "What did you bring us?"

Léon pushed aside the straw and unloaded the rifles hidden in the cart.

"You might want to consider keeping a gun for yourself," Claude offered the priest. "Being a member of the clergy is becoming increasingly dangerous."

Father Jubé smiled. "I have taken a vow against violence. If they come for me, I will not resist."

The maquisard was astonished, "But you have enough munitions to start your own unit!"

"I cannot be directly involved in violence, but indirectly...well, that might be enough to allow me to retain my principles. Remember when we met, the test you gave me? Did God put Adam and Eve in the garden expecting them to avoid the fruit from the Tree of Life, or knowing full well that they would fall and create freewill?"

"I don't even know what you are talking about," Claude replied. "If we can skip the theology lesson, I'd like to take inventory and continue our training?"

"But we've always used Lebels," complained Sister Beatrice, seeing their new rifles. "My father fought with a Lebel."

"It's one of the slowest loading guns in the world," Claude informed her. "Now you use Gewehr 1888s. We can get the ammunition, much easier."

"That's what the Krauts use!" Sister Gabrielle complained.

Léon wanted to explain to them how much easier it would be

to get ammunition for German weapons, but luckily Father Jubé intervened.

"Which makes it easier for us to service and maintain them. Is there anything else you need?" asked, the priest.

"Well, I'd like some panzerknackers," mused Claude. "You know...tank breakers? When I was positioned near Paris, we had S.T. Grenades, but I'd settle for anything we can make into sticky bombs. Food supplies are also appreciated. Every time the Germans send French food to Germany, someone joins the resistance, but we cannot fight without it."

Father Jubé looked at Léon, who was trying to write the list on his hand with a grease pencil. "We will do everything we can. Most of what you have, you can thank to this man's bravery."

Claude looked over the shy thief. "I am Claude Delacroix. Your help is very much appreciated."

Léon was completely taken aback. He was not used to being appreciated. He was not, entirely, sure how to respond. Then he felt something soft touch his shoulder. It startled him as if he had just been caught unaware, yet again. He twisted his neck to find Noele leaning, uncomfortably, close to him as if she didn't want the others to hear what she was about to say. At so close a distance, her black veil could not conceal her youth or beauty. He realized that he had not been so close to a woman, in a great while.

"If you could find some coffee, I would love that. Toasted

barley with chicory isn't really the same. I know it's a small thing, but the things you can't have are the things you miss the most." She looked up and smiled, but when her eyes locked onto his, he felt something seize him inside.

"Yes, of course. I will do my best...I'm Léon, by the way."

"Léon," she repeated. "You're a good man Léon. Merci monsieur."

Now Léon had been called many things in his life, but "good" was not one of them. He felt something, like a breaking wave, envelope him. It was the same sensation he had felt, earlier, when he realized he had been pick-pocketed; and just as disconcerting. He immediately searched his pockets and patted down his pants, but Léon could not alleviate the feeling that something precious was missing. Then, at once, he realized what it was. Someone had stolen his heart.

Klaus slammed the door on his Kübelwagen. He looked at it in distain. "Why doesn't anyone take you? Oh, I know...you're too ugly." With Friedrich not around, he did not feel the need to constrain his feelings towards the vehicle. He turned to walk up to René's door and was astonished to see something, truly beautiful, exiting the mayor's office.

Chloé had the aura of someone who had recently activated their charms, and the effect of her efforts had not yet entirely diminished. She was dressed in the pink and white dress she had used effectively to capture the hearts of all the men in Brassac, before the war. Chloé was a master at substituting for the many shortages such as, using pumice to shave her legs, when razors were no longer available. She smiled at Klaus, not for any particular reason other than she felt it was her duty to charm anyone she encountered.

Positive acknowledgment from the locals, especially from such a beautiful woman, was not something to which Klaus was accustomed. *Perhaps, it was a sign that the locals had accepted their position?* He returned her pleasantries by tipping his black cap, with its unfriendly-looking skull. He knocked twice on the mayor's door and showed himself in.

"Away from the Stapostellen again? I'm beginning to think you like our little town? Don't deny it. You really do!" René was still in an intolerably good mood from his time with Chloé, and even the presence of the Gestapo could not sully his mood.

Klaus smiled in recognition of the mayor's good-natured ribbing, but he was still processing his encounter with the charming Frenchwoman. "Have you heard anything about the trestle?"

"Only that it's being rebuilt, and I've seen quite a few people have been brought in for its reconstruction."

"Yes, it is critical that the line be restored as soon as possible. That said, I must do everything in my power to see that it is not brought down again."

"Of course. Let me know if there's anything I can do," René offered.

Klaus bristled. It was as if his intelligence was being challenged, by such pleasantries. "Oh, that reminds me," he said, producing an arrow from his jacket. "This was found in the head of one of our soldiers. Do you have any idea who might have done such a thing?"

"Americans?" proposed René. "You know, what with the cowboys...and Indians? Not a fan of the cinema? Never mind."

"Do you think it's funny that a German soldier won't be going home?" Klaus, however, was almost reassured by the comment.

The mayor realized he had picked the wrong audience. "Of course not. Actually, many hunters have turned to bow and arrows since rifles were outlawed. It is not at all unusual."

"So what are you saying?" the German wondered.

"Well, it could be almost anyone."

Klaus acknowledged with, "I see," but was not at all happy with his response. Then he recalled meeting Chloé at Chez Honoré, when she had lunched with the mayor. "Are you and the woman who left, just now, intimate?"

René was hardly going to provide the German with such pertinent information. "She is a friend I've known for many years. She's lovely, isn't she? But I suppose you will say that German woman are much prettier?"

"No, quite the contrary. I was just wondering if you would have any objections to my taking the lady out? Since you are only friends, there should be no problem, though?" Klaus knew he had found the fulcrum that would allow him to probe the mayor's loyalties.

René had no desire to see Chloé using her assets to charm the German. He, also, did not know how to prevent such an event from occurring, especially, without tipping his interest in her. "I believe she is just out of a relationship--" he lied.

"Then lunch with a gentleman, such as myself, might be just the thing to soothe her broken heart." Klaus thought he detected René's discomfort, but he would have to pick at the scab longer. "Why don't we let the lady decide?"

René did not respond, but forced a smile and showed Klaus to the door. *Was it not enough that they took Paris from me? Must they take everything beautiful?* His relationship with Chloé, though still in its infancy, had already proven a comfort within his increasingly complicated life.

Claude threw the wine bottles in rapid succession, but the nuns blasted the targets apart, no matter how fast he tossed them. He had hoped to instruct them in how to track and lead a moving target, but it was obvious that their skill was already finely developed. "I'm out of bottles. We're going to have to send Léon to Philippe's yard again."

"Well, it's kind of our hobby. Target shooting, not cleaning up after Philippe."

"Yes," agreed Sister Beatrice. "When you're a teacher, you need to let off a little steam."

"I'm not going to lie," remarked Claude. "You are better shots than I am, but there is more to being a Maquis than knowing your way around a gun. Knowing when and what to fire upon is even more important. Okay, I think that is enough for today."

Noele gathered red currants in her apron while Sister Beatrice read a book of sonnets upon a fallen log. Sister Gabrielle immediately proceeded to use their downtime to do pushups while Sister Dominique helped, in her way, by resting a heavy foot on her back. Every time Gabrielle's head came back down, Robespierre licked her face to help keep her refreshed.

"Where did you learn to fire a gun like that?" Claude asked Marie, wiping his brow.

"My father used to take me hunting. I was very active as a

young girl. I probably would have joined the army, if I were a man. I rather fancy a life of discipline and service."

"Is that so?" remarked Claude. "It never occurred to me, but what you ladies do is not so different--"

"I wasn't always happy with my choice," she reflected. "There was a time when I even thought of leaving the nunnery."

This was something Claude had never heard before; a nun speaking of her regrets. "Is that true?"

"Father Jubé and I had an argument, and I was still young and headstrong. Sister Beatrice saw me packing and said, 'you can't quit now,' and I asked, 'why not?' She said, 'We have gun club today.' It was a lie, of course. They simply rounded up some old hunting rifles and we've been doing it ever since." She smiled at Sister Beatrice who returned the sentiment, oblivious to what could have caused her to be acknowledged so dearly.

Claude heard the sound of the wagon returning and checked his watch. "They have returned to collect the guns."

Léon arrived with the cart and a broad smile. The sisters loaded their weapons back onto it and covered them with hay.

"Where is Father Jubé?" asked Marie.

Léon looked at her, slightly, guilty. "I'm sorry, but he is busy, and I offered to collect the weapons for him."

"That's very kind of you," remarked Noele. "Would you like a berry?"

"Thank you." Léon threw it in the air and caught it in his mouth.

Claude adjusted his beret and sauntered up to him, to have a better look at his new associate. "I was going to ask the good Father something, but since you are here I might as well ask you. We don't have a Eureka, so sometimes we might have to guide Allied planes ourselves if we ever get the chance. Would you be interested in being part of a reception committee if they ever get us supplies?"

"Oui, but of course," Léon replied. "Anything I can do for Brassac." He finished making sure that the rifles had been properly hidden. "Well, I'm afraid I must be off. À plus tard."

As he watched Léon drive away, Claude wondered, "What sort of man is he?"

"He has quite a reputation," Sister Marie observed. "But Father Jubé is very fond of him."

Sister Noele nibbled on one of the berries and added, "And he is very...brave."

"I am so pleased you agreed to have lunch with me," Klaus said with a smile, as he poured Chloé another glass of champagne. "This is from my private collection. Chef Honoré's selection is rather lacking; I'm afraid." He wore his dress uniform, but with a napkin around his neck and having left his hat, he almost appeared like the other patrons at the restaurant.

Chloé watched astonished as the bubbles danced in her glass. Such a luxury was unheard of, and she would have gladly given Mussolini a massage for such an indulgence.

Seeing the struggle of principles he had created, Klaus added, "Oh, I nearly forgot. I brought some chocolates for dessert."

She was used to the maneuverings of local suitors, but Chloé felt as if her emotions were being blitzkrieged. "Monsieur Klaus, it is my pleasure, but why me?"

He looked at her as if it should be obvious. "Clearly you are the most beautiful woman in Brassac. I am of the opinion that if I am going to take someone to lunch, then surely I deserve to be accompanied by you?" He wiped the corners of his mouth with his napkin. "I'm afraid I can't be long. There's a matter with an Allied pilot I must attend to."

"Really?" Chloé marveled, impressed. "How positively fascinating!"

Klaus knew exactly what he was doing, by seeing that such information was widely disseminated. "We're having him transferred from Toulouse to your local hospital tomorrow. So much paperwork, but then your René must, also, have such troubles?"

Chloé blushed, "Well...he's not exactly 'my René,' and I'm sure the problems in such a small town are not nearly as exciting."

Provincial girls are so easily swayed, thought Klaus. It had only taken, but one lunch to cause her to redefine the nature of her relationship with the mayor. "I do hope we can do this again sometime?"

"Mais oui," she replied, and allowed him to take her hand and lift her from her seat. She started to exit the restaurant, when she realized she had forgotten her handbag.

"That's okay, I really need to go," Klaus replied. "Let us say goodbye here?" He kissed her hand and walked outside.

Chloé turned to find Chef Honoré holding her bag. "Merci," she said and tried to take it from him, but he held it tight.

"What?" she exclaimed. "Did the gentleman forget to pay?"

"He never pays," replied Chef Honoré, as he released it. "What are you doing?"

Chloé was astonished to be addressed, in such a way, by a man who was barely an acquaintance. They had spoken many times before, but only with the familiarity that was required of everyone who lives in such a small town. "René and I are not even serious," she protested.

"Not that," he replied. "He's a German!"

"So?" Chloé replied. "And that is none of your business. I will have lunch with whomever I choose. I don't see you turning down their business."

Chef Honoré threw down his apron. "Do you think I have a choice?"

Outside, but within earshot, Friedrich listened carefully and played with his dagger. He did not like the Frenchman's attitude towards the lady, nor his countrymen. No, he did not approve of it, one bit.

CHAPTER ELEVEN
PICK A NUMBER

"Sister Dominique," whined Margot, a feisty ten-year-old who had been her student since her family fled from Reims, "why do we have to do this? It hurts!" She put down her bow and rubbed her sore shoulder. Hugo, who had developed a recent crush on her, smirked and demonstrated his ability to place a bolt at the center of the target.

Sister Dominique helped her hold the arrow behind the fletching. She used her foot, with her own, to provide her with the correct stance. "Archery teaches eye-hand coordination and focus. Focus is everything in education."

"But it hurts my arm."

"Getting stronger hurts," replied Sister Gabrielle.

"Yes, you should only worry if you feel nothing," added Sister Beatrice.

"But don't pull too much draw weight," corrected Sister Dominique.

"Sister, her bow arm is dropping--"

Margot's eyes had started to well. "I'm hungry. Why isn't there anything to eat?"

Hugo put down his bow and pulled something from his pocket. "I found these strawberries. They're already clean." They were quite small, however, having been picked too soon. Hugo swaggered up, with the type of bravado that comes with being ten, "I like archery. Sister Beatrice...when will I be old enough to kill something?"

The question was difficult to hear, for it revealed to her that the war exerted more influence, on her students than even she might. "To even ask such a question is to miss the mark." Sister Beatrice knew that, unlike the other sisters, she was approaching the winter of her years. Her only desire was to finish the race honorably, but perhaps now even that was in doubt. "Ask when you'll be old enough to save someone...or don't ask anything at all."

Philippe was in, especially, good spirits as he accompanied Friedrich to Chez Honoré. When they had reached the entrance, he smiled, for the first time, since the war. "I have always wanted to eat here, but I've never been able to afford it. This will be a real treat!"

Friedrich saw that several soldiers had already positioned themselves outside, expectant of their arrival. "We are not here to dine. If you want to be a milicien, put this on." He handed him a blue beret and jacket. "Now go in there and arrest Chef Honoré."

155

"Chef Honoré? What has he ever done?"

"He has views that are not in line with the new order. Do not worry, the restaurant will only be closed for a short while."

Philippe knew that such a move would, surely, not endear him to the rest of the community. "But I want to join the Service d'ordre légionnaire," protested Philippe.

"It's now the Milice française," Friedrich replied. "Try to keep up."

Philippe smelled something wonderful coming from within the restaurant. "I just want to try their steak tartare. Can't we eat first and then when they give us the chéque--"

Friedrich knew that part of his role was to transform ordinary French civilians into a paramilitary force that could help combat the resistance. He was starting to wonder, however, if he had wasted his time with the particular drunkard whom he had personally recruited. The sounds of a scuffle, from within the restaurant, refocused his attention. He realized that he had lost track of Philippe.

Chef Honoré flew out the door, his apron still covered with sauce, into the waiting arms of the soldiers. "This is outrageous!" he cried. "I'm whisking a hollandaise!"

Friedrich looked up at Philippe, who was panting from having to get physical with the much larger chef. His beret was on sideways and barely rested above his darting eyes. "Welcome to the Milice."

Michel kept his shoulders hunched and his eyes to the ground, as he entered the hospital.

"Michel," someone whispered, not far from the entrance. "Over here." It was a friend he had made through his host family; a French doctor.

"Docteur, thank you so much."

"This should keep you well stocked for months. I'm sorry I couldn't come myself, but we've been very busy lately. Wasn't there anyone else who could come?"

Michel shrugged. "It's okay. Everybody has dysentery, and it's just a hospital."

The doctor looked around, uneasily. "Lately, it's been like Oktoberfest around here. German soldiers...Wehrmacht everywhere."

"Well, that is true all places, these days, no?"

The doctor leaned in close. "There's a British pilot upstairs--" Suddenly, he pushed him in a wheelchair and started to cover his face with bandages.

"What the hell are you doing?" asked Michel. "I'm fine." Then he noticed several German soldiers had come down the stairs. "Um, you're the doctor. You do what seems best."

Friedrich was at the back of the group, holding his hand, and swearing at nobody, in particular. He walked directly up to them, considered Michel for a moment, but then addressed the doctor. "Excuse me, but I seem to have nicked myself coming down the stairs."

"Why, of course, let me have a look," the doctor replied. He turned it over and noted that it did not appear too severe. "I was just doing some bandaging. Let me sterilize it first."

Friedrich looked at Michel, whose face was covered, down to his nose, with thick bandages. "I was playing with my dagger, but let's keep that between us. Dear God, what happened to you?

Michel had preferred not to say anything, lest Friedrich remember their previous encounter. He mumbled, in a lower than regular voice, "I was shot in the eye reporting a member of the resistance."

Perhaps it was too significant a cover-story because Friedrich, immediately, stood at attention. "Gentlemen!" he yelled, calling the other Nazi soldiers. "Herkommen! This man is a national hero. He was injured standing against the Maquis!" The soldiers took turns shaking Michel's limp hand. Friedrich leaned down to him and said, "Now, please don't worry about your infirmity. A great many Germans wear eye-patches, and I must say...the ladies do not mind. Do you know what I'm saying?" Friedrich hit Michel on his left arm, unaware it was where he had previously stabbed him. "It is very dashing."

Michel winced and bit his tongue. "Thank you," he grunted.

The French doctor returned and cleaned Friedrich's cut. "How did you manage to do this?"

"You have a loose nut on the stair railing. It should be inspected before someone gets lockjaw."

"Oh, then I should give you a tetanus shot," concluded the doctor.

Friedrich waited until the bandage was secured. "That won't be necessary. I am in a hurry, and we Germans don't rust. Thank you again and auf wiedersehen."

The doctor waited until the soldiers had left and observed, "There's a loose nut on the stairs, all right." He pushed Michel outside and removed the bandages. "At three o-clock tomorrow, they are transferring the pilot to another hospital not far from Brassac. There's no good reason to do so. Do with this information what you can."

Léon looked into the back of the diesel cargo truck and liked what he saw. Towards its rear was an open box with six, five-hundred gram, blocks labeled "Westfalit." There were also crates of grenades, but they were tightly sealed. Trucks of this type had been more common since the trestle was destroyed. He took note of the Germans nearby, smoking the cheap cigarettes that war had left them, but lost count at twelve men. The situation was not ideal, for if he were caught, sneaking about in the truck's cargo bed, he would be shot or imprisoned. Neither scenario was to his liking. He had decided to simply walk away when he noticed a package labeled, "kaffee." Suddenly, he remembered how Sister Noele had begged him not to have to drink chicory. If there was even a small chance that he might hear, but one kind word from her; then the risk was well worth the gain. He put his shoe on the back of the truck and began to pull himself up.

"Halt! What do you think you are doing?" It was a German with large bushy eyebrows and a small pug nose.

Léon jumped down and brushed himself off. He lifted his index finger as if he was about to say something, but really in an attempt to fabricate a story. "I can't seem to find my watering can." He spoke with the authority of someone who had been in many such similar situations in the past.

One of the German's eyebrows raised, quizzically. "And why would it be in the back of our truck?"

"It's not," Léon laughed. "That would be absurd. No...I thought if I could get up high enough, I'd be able to see it. I'm supposed to water those flowers over there," he pointed to some bushes, near where the other soldiers told a joke at one of their superior's expense.

The soldier looked around. "You are not to be believed. Can't you see it? It's right over there--"

Léon looked across the road and, sure enough, there was a rusty, forlorn water can. He laughed at his good fortune, even if it was an extremely, common object. "Silly me! Well, my eyes aren't so good." He excused himself and started to leave.

"Wait a minute!" cried the German. "I know what you're doing."

"You do?" Léon replied, concerned.

The soldier nodded. "You're over here trying to avoid doing your job. You...are a slacker. Now get that can and water those flowers, immediately, or you'll have to answer to me!"

Léon gulped. "Yes sir, right away." He ran over and retrieved the watering can and felt fortunate to have been so blessed by kismet.

The soldier cracked his thick neck and returned to his friends, but kept a critical eye on Léon until he returned to his "duty" of watering the flowers.

Nothing came from the empty pot, which was no matter as it was all a ruse, anyway. Léon walked over to the house to fill it again, but then a rather better idea struck him. There was an old rubber hose that would suit his scheme, quite nicely. He sauntered to the back of the truck and began to siphon gasoline into the watering pot. When he had filled it, he hid the hose and returned to the rose bushes. Now he began to "water" around the soldiers, creating an invisible perimeter of gasoline. He decided that he had not saturated the ground enough, so he returned to the truck several more times; as he drenched the area with gas.

The German saw that Léon had been about his work for a while and decided to take pity upon him. "Frenchy, come over here. Bitte."

Léon pointed at himself and sulked over to where he now counted fifteen Germans. "Oui?"

The soldier pushed a cigarette in his mouth. "You work hard. I like that." He lit it for him.

"Merci," Léon replied, afraid he might suddenly combust. He waited until he had crossed, outside the perimeter and tossed the cigarette to the ground. Then, as if Hell's ceiling had fractured, fire rose from the ground and encircled the soldiers. Léon jumped into the back of the truck and grabbed the coffee, but paused to smack himself on the forehead. He had, nearly, forgotten the plastic explosives. Five bricks went into his overalls, as he leaped from the truck and sprinted around the corner. There was not enough time to sift through the remaining boxes. *Wait*, he thought. *Weren't there six bricks?* Then he heard the sound of ordnance detonating. "Ah, there were six."

162

René carefully chiseled away at the piece of French walnut, as he encouraged the grain to express itself. The vine that wrapped around the chair's legs looked so real that one could almost expect it to produce wine. He was so engrossed that he had not even noticed Chloé standing behind him, her head resting against the doorframe, hypnotized by his artistry.

"I have not seen you work on anything so delicate in quite some time," she observed. She had only just awoken from the spell his craftsmanship had placed upon her. "Do you actually have an order?"

René laughed and brushed some dust off of one of the leaves. "It's for a very important client...our own Father Jubé, but he does not even know that I am making it for him. Sister Marie said he needed a chair."

"I had no idea such things were made, anymore. People often tell me I am beautiful, but you make things that *are* beautiful."

René smiled. "I have already remade it three times. I try to carve, but then I think of what I want it to be...what it needs to be and just lose all faith in my abilities."

Chloé took it out of his hands and studied the stem that wrapped around its arm. She looked at René with new eyes, unable to imagine how something so fine had been carved by hand. "I looked for you at your office, but I knew I'd find you here."

"The mayor is indisposed," René sighed. "I find it very

comforting here, amongst the tools of my former trade. If I focus hard enough, I can even make the war go away."

Chloé smiled. "I wish you could show me how."

"Now I have become the tool of ironmongers who care nothing for beauty...or truth."

She handed him back the arm piece. "I wanted to tell you something."

"That is not necessary," he replied. "We are adults." He knew what she was about to say, but wished that she would leave it unsaid.

Chloé almost took advantage of the escape route he had provided her, but looked at the chair and decided that she respected him too much not to be forthright. "I went to lunch with Klaus."

René nodded, but continued to focus on his work. "You don't have to ask permission from me. We have never been exclusive then, have we?"

"No," she replied, "but I thought you would like to know."

He took out a piece of sandpaper and pretended not to be bothered by the thought, but his choice of words betrayed him. "If you want to be seen as fraternizing with the Gestapo, then that's your business." He regretted the way the words tasted, even as they left his lips.

Chloé absorbed their bitterness. "How dare you...and who are you to judge me? You're in bed more with the Germans than I could ever hope to be." Her heels clacked against his floor as she passed, close enough to vibrate the sawdust on his desk. The door, slammed and he was left alone with his regret.

René sighed in disgust, and slammed the piece he carved on the table. He knew that she was right, which is the very same reason he avoided the one for whom the chair was intended. Father Jubé would have administered the ceremony if he had married Noele. He had not even done him the honor of explaining himself after he had left for Paris; or since he had returned for that matter. Chloé was their maid of honor, so she knew his transgressions well. There was no point in putting on airs where she was concerned. In truth, he felt he should have better protested Klaus' advances towards her. Now he wondered if it had been more her test, than the German's.

"A pilot?" Sister Anette repeated. "Why would they bring a pilot here? Isn't the hospital at Toulouse much better?"

"Yes, that's what Michel radioed to tell me," agreed Sister Marie. "It's definitely a trap. Maybe, they're hoping to ensnare any local resistance, but we are one step ahead of them."

Sister Dominique, who had been carving arrows, asked, "So, what do you have in mind?"

Marie knew not to table a suggestion unless she, already, had a

165

plan. The sisters were too unpredictable to not have a course prepared. "We will do what they can not anticipate. We will intercept the target before they can transfer him. Then we will escort him to our safe house in Moissac."

Sister Beatrice, who always thought five moves ahead, replied with dread, "Surely, an Allied pilot is important, but we would only risk the safety of all those already hiding. We might deliver a great victory to our enemies by giving them the lives of those they are fighting and those we are trying to protect."

Marie had expected this response and had offered the same protest when Michel first made the suggestion. "Which is why we will fake that the pilot has been killed, trying to escape, and substitute a corpse. They will think the matter is resolved."

"And what is our role?" Sister Anette wondered, afraid of the answer.

"You will meet me at the rendezvous location, on the road the ambulance will take. You will bring the corpse, and we will switch it with the pilot's clothes." She tried to be indifferent as she revealed the next part of her plan. "If, for some reason, I do not make it...assume that the pilot is still en route to Castres, our local hospital. The ambulance must never arrive. If it does, you will not attempt to liberate him, as that is where they will set their ambush."

Sister Noele looked horrified. This was too close to an actual mission and not at all like the usual level of mischief they regularly engaged in. "You talk like it is no small thing that you might not return? What will become of us if something happens?"

Marie did not hold her life cheap, but she observed, "Pilot's are expensive to train and difficult to replace. I don't know this man, but if he can help return the world to a place in which our lives make sense...then I am willing to risk mine saving him."

Robespierre let out a short bark, and the nuns scrambled for their rifles. Claude entered the camp, pushing a wheelbarrow, and gazed up indifferently at the weapons addressed at him. From the uniform, he appeared to be carting a dead German.

"Nice corpse," observed Sister Dominique.

Claude grinned, "Sorry I'm late. Did I miss anything?"

Sister Marie looked at the soldier, who only appeared to be sleeping due to his lack of apparent wounds. "Excellent work. Where did you find such a fresh corpse?"

"Where did I find him?"

"Yes, the dead German," clarified Marie. "He was already dead when you found him, right?"

"Well, he was dead...shortly there afterward."

"Claude!" cried Sister Marie. She threw her hands up and walked away.

Sister Gabrielle picked up the dead man's hand and watched it fall.

"Well, you wanted him to be fresh. There's not a lot of action around here, and it was getting late." The maquisard was not used to having to explain himself.

"He does look kind of British," offered Sister Dominique.

"Yes, I'm quite happy with him," reflected Claude. "I think he'll do nicely--"

Friedrich threatened Chef Honoré with wolfish eyes, their cold intensity as effective a device as his dagger.

"I've done nothing. Now I need to get back to my restaurant. I have a beef stock on the burner. Let me make you something? Something special!"

"Thank you, but I have already had käsespätzle with a nice Riesling." Friedrich signaled for two members of the French Gestapo to position him against the wall.

Chef Honoré exuded fear in the form of perspiration. "Am I under arrest? What are the charges?"

"You are under protective custody. There are many who say you have been speaking against Germany's attempts to help France. My job is to see that no harm comes to you. After all...many of your countrymen, such as Philippe here, do not take treason so lightly."

Chef Honoré started to tremble. "Philippe. Tell them that I am harmless! Tell them how people rely upon me. Help me Philippe!"

Friedrich smiled and for a moment his tone mimicked that of his superior, whom he attempted to emulate. "This is a new experience. I have never seen a traitor plead his case to a member of the Milice! Should I call the Führer so you can talk with him as well?"

"What do you want?" Chef Honoré pleaded. "I am ready to help you! Please give me a chance!"

Friedrich squinted his eyes and tried to get a sense of the chef's sincerity. "I need to know why my countrymen keep showing up dead? With so many people coming to your restaurant, you must hear things?"

"Yes, I hear things. What do you want to know?"

Friedrich tilted his cap in an attempt to mimic Klaus. "Who is so talented with a bow and has such an inclination for mischief?"

Philippe leaned forward, for he had started to form opinions of his own. He had not the courage to give voice to them as his heart was a torrent of conflict and self-loathing.

Now Chef Honoré started to waver, but he realized any attempt to save himself would only bring death upon another. His first thoughts rested upon the sisters, but if he were to die, he did not want to have to explain himself.

Friedrich gave him a moment to wrestle with his conscience, a condition with which he had no personal experience. "Perhaps I can help you...there is a game I like to play with my dagger--"

Chef Honoré looked at the sharp, brown implement of Friedrich's cruelty, and his last shred of will was severed. *No*, he thought. *I will have to tell them about the sisters.* "I have something to tell you--"

Just then, Klaus strode up, relieved, to have finally found Friedrich. He seemed quite put out and in a rush. He looked at the small collection of Gestapo and Milice and exclaimed, "Really, Friedrich, I've been looking everywhere for you! I need you to get back to Toulouse and oversee the transfer of the special prisoner. We don't have time for cutlery games!"

"My apologies Herr Klaus, but I only need a moment."

Klaus sighed and pulled out his Luger. He pointed it at the prisoner and said, "Pick a number between one and ten."

"Seven," the chef stammered.

There was a high-pitched crack, like that of a steel whip, and Chef Honoré dropped where he stood. Klaus holstered his Luger and turned, nonchalantly, to Friedrich. "Alright, then...let's go. Kommen sie jetzt!"

Friedrich followed like a dog brought to heel, but then stopped; having remembered something. "Wait...what was the number?"

"The what?"

"You know, the one you asked him to pick."

Klaus searched his memory for a second, but then laughed. "You know, I completely forgot to pick one."

Philippe ran up to them, completely out of breath and in a state of shock, from what he had just seen. "The man you shot...that was Chef Honoré!"

Klaus looked at the Frenchman, perplexed for a moment like he might admonish him, but then replied, "Was it? I completely didn't recognize him without his hat. Damn it! I loved his soupe au pistou. Well, I'm sure he left the recipe lying about somewhere."

Klaus led Friedrich down a small country trail, but then stopped and doubled back to the fork in the road, they had just passed. "Well, this can't be it--"

"What?" asked Friedrich.

"Where the hell did I park the car?"

CHAPTER TWELVE
BAIT AND SWITCH

It was not yet quite a chair, but it had started to take the form of one. More than that, René now comprehended how the heart was the real tool for transforming even the most mundane object into art. He ran his thumb along the scroll work and admitted that he had never made so fine a piece for a paying customer. It was as if all the artistic energy that had been pent up, since the beginning of the war, had been lavished on this singular object. It was clear that the many hours of meditative craftsmanship had not been, merely, a physical application of carpentry, but an attempt at personal redemption.

The light inside his workshop was sufficient for making toys and farm tables, but not for something so intricate that it appeared to breathe. Outside, the highly-figured wood shown, spectacularly, under the soft provincial sun; and the grain revealed the fingerprints of its creator. The chair's craftsman did not see that its intended recipient gazed upon him like a religious icon.

Father Jubé was oblivious to the fact that he had any connection to the object, which he admired from over the mayor's shoulder. He did not want to startle him, so he waited until his chisel lifted before he asked, "Why hello René, what are you working on?"

René spun around and attempted to block the priest's view. "Just a little something to keep my hands busy." He threw a blanket over the chair and pretended to brush off the wood dust.

"Don't be coy," Father Jubé admonished him. "I know exactly what you're doing."

René began to perspire, as had been his custom when he was his student. He had a poor record of being shifty around the priest. The chair was meant to express the things he could not say.

"You're making furniture for your office." Father Jubé tried to look under the blanket, but René intercepted him. "Well, I suppose it's appropriate for the mayor to have accessories commiserate with his position. I'm sorry we could not provide you with a better desk and chairs--"

René exhaled, relieved that his surprise had not been discovered. "Well, I guess Paris rubbed off on me? Is there something I can help you with?"

Father Jubé used his index finger to brush his nose. "Say...René, do you remember when you first came to our school?"

"Not really. I was just a young boy."

The priest nodded. "Well, I remember. I remember like it was yesterday. We had just finished painting the classroom, and I was absolutely covered--"

"I was scared," René interrupted, "but you made me feel like everything was going to be okay...like you always have. That's what I remember...a feeling that I was safe." He wiped his chisel against his apron.

"Yes...good. I am happy you felt that way, but now it seems the time has come for us to change roles." Father Jubé now became, uncharacteristically, forthright. "René, my position has become a perilous one. Would you promise me something?"

"Anything."

"If something should happen to me, would you watch over Sister Marie?"

René was not sure how to respond. Here was the person who had always held the planets in order, asking him to protect the strongest person in Brassac. Surely, she was the least likely person to need his help, but he could hardly refuse a request from Father Jubé. "You have my word, but why me?"

The priest seemed to speak from a distance. "Age has given me the humility to know when my students have surpassed me. It is the one consolation time has provided."

"Don't be ridiculous," René protested. "Maybe the others, but I know that, surely, I have been a disappointment."

Father Jubé put his hand on his shoulder. "René, you are wrong. Don't you not know that I have a parent's blindness? I only see the good things you do, and I am *very* proud."

The mayor could not accept his mercy. "You know...you've never asked me about Noele. You, of all people, understand how she came to the convent--"

"René, what I know is how you struggle. If you did not struggle, *then* would I worry. If you resigned yourself to your circumstances and moral failings, *then* would I despair."

"Why are you telling me these things?" His face, riddled with worry, René pressed for further elucidation. "Something must be wrong. What aren't you telling me?"

"I too am engaged in a struggle and it is almost time to teach my last lesson." The priest hoisted himself back up, onto the seat of his mule cart.

"And what is that?" asked René.

"Winning is not justice and the truth can never be defeated."

"Why again am I dressed like a nun?" Claude looked both perplexed and galled, as he stood in his second-hand habit. In the sister's defense, he didn't look any more mannish than some of the nuns they had met at their conference in Lourdes.

Sister Marie looked him over and was well satisfied with her work. "If a man were spotted alone in the woods, with a group of nuns, it might appear odd."

"And this is your solution?" He had dressed as a priest, once before, but this stretched the boundaries of propriety. "I am definitely going to Hell for this."

Sister Gabrielle eyed him over and thought he looked the part quite well. "Don't worry...we'll put in a good word for you." All the sisters laughed, relieved to have an excuse to have some fun at his expense.

Marie knew she needed to demonstrate confidence though she was not without reservations. If she were caught, she would surely be thrown into prison. "Brother Léon will drive Sister Noele, and I, to Toulouse. We'll see the rest of you at the twelve kilometer mark, where we'll switch the body. Claude...I mean Sister Claudette, will help you make the preparations. Follow his directions to the letter."

"But he looks ridiculous," Sister Beatrice groused. "How can I take him serious?"

Steam could almost be seen coming from his ears. "That's it; I'm changing!"

Sister Marie grabbed his shoulder. "You'll listen to him like he's Joan of Arc herself." Then she looked Claude straight in the eye, "I never wanted to be anything, but a soldier of the heart, but sometimes a nun has to become a soldier and a soldier a nun."

"Where? Where does it say that?" asked an exasperated Claude, as Sister Gabrielle adjusted his coif.

"I'm paraphrasing."

Claude looked at each of the sisters and thought about how

much they had changed since he first met them on the trestle; a silvery moon, casting shadows off of their monochromatic figures. He now believed that they were capable of such a complex mission. Surely, such a change had occurred because each of them had been willing to abandon a piece of themselves. "Alright then. The rest of us will have to work fast, to be ready in time for the ambulance. Sisters Marie and Noele, who has some background in nursing, will be on board, and they are counting on us."

"How will we know we are at the rendezvous point to stop the ambulance?" asked Sister Noele.

"Don't worry," replied Sister Marie. "Claude and I have worked out a plan."

"Yes, our team will bury three rows of rocks in the road. When you feel the bumps, you will tell the ambulance driver you need him to pull over. Tell him it is essential that you stop immediately. We will be waiting to ambush--"

"Is that when we switch the kraut?" asked Sister Anette.

Claude looked under the blanket to see how the slowly, decomposing German soldier was doing. "Yes, we will switch him for the British pilot and light the ambulance on fire. Is everyone clear on the plan?"

"The pilot will never reach Brassac." Sister Marie looked at the old pocket watch she often carried. "Now where is Léon? We have a very specific window to get to the hospital."

Toot. Toot. Everyone turned to find Léon, driving up in Klaus' stolen Kübelwagen. He tossed a package of coffee at Noele. "All aboard for Toulouse."

The German R75 motorcycle backfired as it came to a stop outside the hospital. Klaus tried to look dignified as he lifted himself out of the sidecar. Friedrich removed his dust goggles and hopped off of the bike that was attached physically, and metaphorically, to his Obersturmbannführer.

"It's not that I don't trust any of these idiots...it's just that I don't trust any of these idiots!" Klaus went over and took note of the ambulance that would transport the pilot. "They were planning on using a green military ambulance with an escort. This is better. The resistance would never attack a civilian ambulance."

Friedrich brushed dust from his black, leather riding coat. "Perhaps, I should ride along with the driver?"

Klaus rolled his eyes, pointedly. "You're rather well-known around Brassac now, aren't you? No, I'll send a member of the Gestapo, dressed as a civilian. Now let's be sure to review all the arrangements inside. I'm pretty sure my lunch had a higher IQ than the people you've installed here."

"We're just outside town, and the hospital is only a block further, on the left," Léon explained. He appeared shiftier than normal. If he was jittery, it was from being so close to civilization in a stolen vehicle. He had brought a German hat to make himself passable to anyone who didn't take a second glance.

"You're the best Léon." Sister Noele kissed him on the cheek and jumped out of the car.

Léon was a glacier until, all at once, his cynicism calved. Over the sound of his crashing indifference, he heard Sister Marie.

"You'd better scoot now," she said. "This vehicle is obviously stolen and you look about as much a Nazi as Churchill. Another thing, ditch this thing immediately. We were blessed to have made it this far. Walk back, if you have to." Sister Marie placed her hand on his shoulder, which could be interpreted as either a wish for good luck or a gesture of farewell.

"Oui, I can do that," replied Léon. "They'll never find it."

René had stenciled a script on the cresting rail, which he prepared to carve. There were plenty of matters worthy of his attention, back at his office, but completing the chair had become his passion. A clanging, bell-like sound caught his attention, and he looked up to find Philippe, a bottle of wine in one hand and two more tightly gripped in the other. He swayed back and forth, in a way that reminded him of a pendulum, as he used every inch of the road's width.

"Philippe. Hé là...Philippe!" The mayor knew that Philippe was technically breaking the law, being outside in such a condition, but prosecuting individuals with such powerful friends was a delicate matter. It was just as well, as René rather preferred to reason with him, anyway.

Philippe glared, in the way that only a disgruntled drunkard could accomplish. "Well, if it isn't Monsieur Maires de Brassac? What do you want? I'm quite busy." He slurred his words in a way that reeked of Bordeaux and disgust.

René put down his tools and straightened his back. "Now don't be cross with me. That's the wine talking or is something else the matter?"

"Chef Honoré is dead."

René was nonplussed. "So, I've heard. I didn't know you were that close."

Phillipe looked for a moment like he might assault him. "I never even ate there, but now...I sure as hell won't!"

René was a regular, but he had decided to bury his emotions lest Klaus notice and draw conclusions that were not politically appropriate. "So, is that what upsets you? You're mourning the loss of his cuisine?"

"Imbécile." Philippe would have had trouble articulating his feelings, even sober.

"Then, you're upset about the way it happened?" René wanted to help Philippe; if for no other reason than he seemed about to implode psychologically.

"Je ne sais pas." Philippe had no idea what he felt.

"You're upset with yourself?"

Philippe didn't reply, but he didn't need to. He fell on his bottom, in the middle of the road, and guzzled the rest of the bottle.

"Now Philippe. I really doubt that is going to help, or I would have sought out that solution long ago. Have you--"

"--gone to Sister Marie? Don't bother."

"I was going to say Father Jubé." He had forgotten that Sister Marie was to Philippe, what Father Jubé had always been to him.

Philippe hurled the bottle down the road, which scattered glass shards, like a firework of dejection. He looked like he was going to sob, but he just heaved quietly; without tears.

René walked over and put his arm around him. "You know, I believe you might have come to the right place." He coyly slipped the two remaining bottles out of Philippe's hands. "Father Jubé says we make our own prisons, well I've decided to find a way out. What do you say, Philippe? Let's find our way out together?" A car door slammed, a bit further down the road. René watched Chloé, flirt with some low-ranking German soldiers, perhaps to increase his jealousy or possibly oblivious to his presence. "When this is over. I don't want to have to convince myself that I was just doing what I had to. Surviving isn't enough anymore for me, anymore. I'm ashamed if it ever was."

Claude looked at his "nunified" reflection in the puddle and thought, *Sacrebleu! What has become of me?* He had prepared the sisters for survival, but his personal transformation was one fraught with peril. Where once he acted out of pure instinct, now he caught himself weighing issues of morality. He peeked under the gray wool blanket, which covered the dead German, and wondered what sort of man he had been. Maybe he wasn't even a Nazi? Maybe he was just a Bavarian farmer or a conscripted factory worker? These were not the thoughts of a Maquis, but perhaps the nuns had started to wear off on him. *Did it even matter?* He would not have acted any differently; though he had the chance. If he had been forced to kill, it was because the Nazis had put him in that position. Claude wondered why his thoughts were so troubled while the nuns moved through such times with ease? When he had met them, he had assumed that the context of war was more his element, but it was they who had helped him understand its true nature. For what was war, but a moral argument where one party tried to win through force? The nuns had shown him that decisions of conscience reverberated long after the cannons stilled.

A splinter, from one of the wheelbarrow's wooden handles, irritated his palm. He was about to ask someone to relieve him, when Robespierre, stopped and let out a short bark. Claude heard the familiar sound of boots that trampled the gravel of a country road.

Two Germans appeared from, seemingly nowhere, but apparently a camouflaged nest. "Halt!" cried one of the soldiers, who displayed his hand.

Claude winced and realized that he had become so engaged in his postulations, that he had totally missed the gleam of steel from within the foliage. The wheelbarrow slipped from his hands and teetered until it nearly spilled its contents. One of the corpse's arms became free and dangled. Sister Gabrielle tried to stuff it, nonchalantly, back under the blanket, but it was stiff and resisted.

"What is your business?" asked one of the soldiers, in passable French. He had a duster mustache that made him look more like a grotesquely large version of Charlie Chaplin than Hitler.

Claude coughed, in an attempt to encourage one of the nuns to say something, rightfully, concerned that it might give away their ruse if he spoke; with his masculine voice. He nudged Sister

183

Anette, whose eyes moved like she was in the REM stage of sleep. It did not serve their goal of appearing inconspicuous. Now he noticed a third soldier, who lay prone on the ground and manned an MG-42 machine gun; better known as "Hitler's Buzzsaw" from the terrible sound it made. He had heard its song before, and he thought it brought to mind Hell's zipper being ripped open to receive him.

Robespierre barked incessantly at the other soldier, who had steel-gray eyes and beard stubble that appeared like a thousand pin needles were trying to escape from his face.

"What's in the wheelbarrow?" asked the soldier with the mustache. "Tell me...are you really nuns or smuggling black market trade?"

Sister Beatrice tried to covertly block their view. "Why does everyone always ask us that? Of course, we're nuns! Would you like us to recite the Mass in Latin?"

"Honestly, didn't your mothers teach you any manners?" Sister Gabrielle added.

"Well--" stammered the soldier.

Claude marveled that their robes seemed to be paying off.

The steely-eyed German had enough of Robespierre's yapping, however. "Someone better shut that dog up, or I'm going to put a hole in him."

Sister Dominique's hand went to her rifle, which was hidden

under her habit. "That would be a bad call."

"Let me have a look under that blanket," instructed the other soldier. "I'd better check...then you can be on your way."

Sister Anette had finally found her voice. "Those are just potatoes."

His partner, however, addressed his gun at Robespierre and gave him a look that dared him to bark.

Behind the wheelbarrow Claude, slowly, reached for his pistol, but before he had time to act Sister Dominique's skirt flew up. Both her bloomers and her sawed-off Gewehr 1888 rifle were revealed. There was a flash and the soldier, who had been so eager to shoot Robespierre, flew back. Claude took the other soldier's stunned reaction to fire three rounds into him.

"Run!" cried Sister Beatrice. They dropped the wheelbarrow and fled for the cover of the forest.

The ripping sound of the MG-42, in the nest, confirmed that the soldier there had accurately appraised the situation. The first burst, of what would amount to 1,800 rounds per minute, stirred the road and created a sizable dust storm. The nuns jumped into the foliage, lay flat on their stomachs, and waited for a pause from the deadly hail.

"Is everyone alright?" asked Sister Beatrice.

"They got me," cried Sister Anette.

Beatrice examined her apron, but the only holes she found had passed, safely, through her skirt. "You're fine...it went straight through the cloth."

Anette sighed in relief. "Yes, but I was still, technically, shot."

"Well," snapped Sister Beatrice at Dominique. "I think we could have handled that differently." Pieces of bark rained from the trees as bullets tore them apart.

"Robespierre doesn't think so," she replied.

Sister Gabrielle noticed that the barking had stopped. "Where is he, anyway? Has anyone seen Robespierre?"

Sister Dominique leaned back, but the sound of the machine gun proved deafening. "Don't worry, he's delivering something for me."

"What's he delivering?"

There was a small explosion and the MG-42 fell silent.

The dust settled, and they could hear Robespierre's paws scurrying along, unseen. Then he appeared, through the beige cloud, carrying the head of the German gunner in his mouth.

Claude leaned over, from around the tree, and observed, "There's something not right about that dog."

Léon put a large rock on the brake pedal of the Kübelwagen. It had served them well, in its limited goal of delivering Sister

Marie and Noele to Toulouse. Now it was a liability that was just as likely to get him killed. He shuffled over to the edge of the small cliff and peered down. It wasn't the most remote place to dispose of a stolen vehicle, but it would have to serve its purpose. Naturally, a small pond would have been preferable, but it was too risky to drive the Kübelwagen any closer to town.

He looked around for a large rock and wondered how the nuns faired? The Kübelwagen was a better car than any he had ever owned, and it seemed a shame to have to destroy it. The daily waste of war grated on him. Noele's pursuit to become a nun, well that seemed just as unfortunate.

Léon placed the other rock on the car's accelerator pedal, and the Kübelwagen bucked against its brakes. He didn't really want to do it, never having owned a car. *Such a waste...such a waste*, he thought, but driving around in a German personnel vehicle was, hardly, a viable solution. Léon stood safely outside the door and lifted the stone that held the brake pedal. The Kübelwagen rocketed towards the edge of the cliff, hung suspended in mid-air, and then disappeared. He covered his ears, expecting the impact, but nothing happened.

After a minute, Léon walked to the edge and peered down. The Kübelwagen had come to rest, high atop some trees. It wasn't the most permanent solution, but it was unlikely anyone would find it in time for it to cause them any difficulties. *Who knows,* thought Léon. *Maybe I'll come back, after the war, and retrieve it for myself?*

"Well, there's the ambulance, but how do we get in the back of it?" Toulouse's hospital seemed intimidating and metropolitan to Noele, who rarely left Brassac. Still, it was a relief to have come so far. Eventually, however, they would have to step out from behind their cover and risk discovery.

Sister Marie looked about and wondered which personnel worked for the hospital and which were Gestapo. I hope Michel was able to get our message to his friend--" A hand placed itself on her shoulder, and she spun around to see Noele strike its owner on the jaw.

"Wait, it's me! I'm the doctor...Michel's friend." He tried to get off his knees, but stumbled back to the ground.

Noele stopped herself short of following up with a devastating hook, cross combination.

"Thank goodness we left the guns at home," she admonished Noele.

The doctor kept a wary eye on her and allowed Sister Marie to steady him. "The pilot is being taken to the ambulance. You'll only have a few minutes to intercept him."

"Tell us what we need to do," Sister Marie implored him.

He pointed to the hospital's garden. "I've left a window open to his room on the second floor. There's a ladder in the rose bushes. The nurse, watching him is Gestapo. You will have to eliminate her if you are to escort the pilot."

"Then they are only expecting one nurse?"

The doctor was a meticulous gentleman, who had already anticipated the problem. "I've listed two nurses on the manifest. Here are the uniforms and your hospital identification papers. Please change here."

Sister Marie waited for him to turn around.

"Really, sister. I'm a doctor."

"And I'm a nun. Turn around."

The doctor mumbled something, in French. "I will meet you at the ambulance If the gurney, with the pilot, is not down there at the correct time; we will certainly have trouble."

Noele was still adjusting her nurse's uniform as she ran to catch up to Sister Marie, who had already positioned the ladder under the window. Through the window, Marie saw a severe-looking woman who was checking the restraints on a patient. She assumed it was their pilot and, although, he had a few cuts and bruises he appeared otherwise, healthy.

"Don't move or even speak," the nurse instructed him, "or I will torture you all the way to Castres." She had not noticed Sister

189

Marie peeking through the window. "I really was a nurse, so I know just how to make it hurt."

The pilot, however, had noticed someone by the window and tried to offer her assistance. "Can you get me a glass of water?"

The nurse balked. "I should think you'd be more amiable if your were thirsty?"

"I promise I won't complain, if I could just have a drink."

It seemed a simple enough request to make her job easier. She glared at the pilot, but went into the bathroom to get a glass.

Sister Marie and Noele leaped through the window. As the nurse exited, Marie struck her in the head with Corporal Punishment. The nurse fell, but came back swinging. Sister Noele blocked an uppercut and lay her flat with a hook to the temple.

"Where on earth did you learn to fight like that?" asked Sister Marie.

"Two brothers," Noele replied.

The pilot looked at them confused, but relieved. "Who in bloody hell are you?"

"Just a couple nuns...well I'm in training," clarified Noele.

"Whatever, get me out of here," he strained against the straps. "They're about to transfer me somewhere, no doubt unpleasant."

Sister Marie got behind the gurney and pushed him towards the door.

"You're going the wrong way," he protested.

"If they don't see you get into that ambulance, we'll never get you out of here."

To the pilot, Marie sounded positively mad. "I think I'd rather take my chance with the Gestapo hag."

As they exited the room, Friedrich was there to meet them. "Just one minute," he said, stopping the gurney. He checked his manifest and said, "Let me see your papers." Marie handed him the paperwork that the doctor had provided them. "Fine...sehr gut." He held his dagger under the pilot's cheek. "Now don't you give these ladies any trouble. They are not regular nurses, you know?"

"Well," replied the pilot. "I'm certainly aware they are not to be trifled with."

Friedrich looked at the pilot curiously, but couldn't grasp the duality of his meaning. "Put him in the ambulance," he barked. He wasn't, entirely, sure if the pilot was being cooperative or had attempted to mock him.

Léon peddled back to the church on a stolen, rusty bicycle to find Father Jubé waiting for him. "It's all done. They're at the hospital, and the car has been disposed of."

A look of relief overcame the priest, but then he noticed Léon's latest mode of transportation. "And you will return the bicycle, no?"

The thief sighed. "I just nearly died. What ever happened to judge not?"

"Really Léon? Are you going to misuse the very words I taught you? Are you suggesting we not judge the Nazis either? If that is supposed to be an instruction to ignore evil...then everything we have done is for naught." Father Jubé seemed to contemplate this a moment, and then added, "Only God can save the sisters now, and I'm not about to let a bicycle stand in our way."

CHAPTER THIRTEEN
HELP FROM ABOVE

"Who's on my foot?" cried Sister Anette. An evergreen shrub poked inside one of her nostrils. They were bunched as tight as kindling, so that no one could tell who was upon whom.

Sister Dominique squirmed and stammered. "Maybe if the bolt of your rifle wasn't jabbing me--"

"We should have let them have their rifles," protested Sister Anette. "What if they were caught? Maybe the ambulance isn't coming?"

"They had to climb into a second story window," Claude objected, defending his plan. The truth of the matter was that he had been second-guessing himself for the last hour. "And what if they were searched? What then?"

"Robespierre just licked me," Beatrice complained, in a tone laced with disgust.

"So?" Sister Dominique didn't think her dog was being given enough credit for his role, thus far. Especially, after he had delivered a grenade to the gunnery nest.

"He touched a Nazi with that mouth. It's not sanitary."

The nuns began to bicker, but then hushed themselves. For a few moments, only the wind whistled through the oak-hornbeam trees.

"We'll know soon enough," observed Sister Beatrice. "The ambulance should pass here any minute."

Sister Gabrielle started to leave their cover. "I want to check the stones again. Maybe, we buried them too deep?"

"Stay where you are...they're fine," Claude grabbed her by her veil. "Haven't you ever ridden in an ambulance? They'll feel it."

Robespierre's bat-like ears stood at attention, and he let out an anxious whine.

"He hears something," Sister Dominique informed them. "Someone's coming!"

The ambulance moved like an inchworm, its nose bobbing up and down with each dip in the road. Then it shuttered, as it passed over the three lines of rocks they had planted. This was to be the signal, to Sister Marie and Noele, that they were at the ambush point. Claude and the nuns watched, expectantly, for it to come to a stop. They knew Marie would take any measures necessary to get their driver to pull over, even if it meant opening the doors to the ambulance.

"Why isn't it stopping?" asked Sister Anette, voicing what the others were already thinking. "Maybe with the road...they can't tell the difference?"

Claude was mute, but only because he was still weighing his options. *Maybe it's moving slow enough that we can ambush it?*

Then he watched as the road became smooth, and the ambulance accelerated. It passed, almost, out of sight before he even had a chance to react.

Then, something happened that none of them could have anticipated. The trees moved as if a giant grabbed hold of them and shook, vigorously. The ambulance came to an immediate stop and its back end lifted off the ground, then slammed down again. There was the sound of glass shattering, and smoke poured from the ambulance.

"Let's go!" Claude cried, as he sprang from their cover with his pistol.

The back doors of the ambulance flung open, and Sister Marie leaped out. She grabbed the gurney, the pilot still strapped to it, and began to pull. Meanwhile, the driver stumbled from the cab, blood dripping from his forehead. He saw the nuns, a dog, and a wheelbarrow that seemed to move on its own; pushed by a hunched over Sister Gabrielle. As he tried to process the situation, Sister Marie walked up from behind him, with Capital Punishment, and turned out his lights.

"The whole thing is on fire. Somebody help me get this thing down from here!" Sister Noele had been left alone for a moment, as Sister Marie took care of the driver. The gurney rested, half-way, in the back of the ambulance. Sisters Anette and Beatrice took over and helped lower it to the ground.

"Would somebody get me out of this damn thing?" yelled the pilot, still restrained, and aware of the fire.

Claude examined his restraints. "It's locked. I guess they didn't want you going anywhere. I'm afraid I'll have to shoot it." Before the pilot had any time to object, Claude pulled out his pistol and blasted the lock apart. Sister Marie helped him remove the leather straps, and he toppled to the ground.

"Take off your clothes," Sister Gabrielle instructed.

"I beg your pardon?" replied the pilot.

Sister Marie lifted the blanket, to reveal the German corpse; they had brought. "Here's your change of wardrobe. We haven't much time."

"Couldn't you at least have undressed him? He's kind of manky."

Claude let out a short, dismissive laugh. "And how were we to explain pushing around a dead, naked German? Help me strap him to the gurney. He's going to be you."

The pilot undressed, which revealed several nasty bedsores on his back. Sister Gabrielle handed him the German's clothes whom she, likewise, dressed in the pilot's hospital gown.

"Now I look like a bloody German! What if the resistance sees me?"

"Relax Brit," said Claude. "I'm not going to shoot you."

Each of the nuns grabbed a corner of the gurney and lifted the corpse, now dressed to resemble the pilot, back into the ambulance.

"They'll think you've died in the crash and hopefully that will buy us some time to get you out of here." Sister Marie was fairly pleased with the plan they had fabricated. She had been so busy carrying out its details, however, that she had completely forgotten to determine what had caused the ambulance to halt, so suddenly.

The pilot, though, had walked to the front of the ambulance and proceeded to offer some clarification. "Bloody hell! Did that car fall onto us from those trees?" The Kübelwagen sat upside down, on the cab of the ambulance. It had started a fire that was, quickly, consuming both vehicles. Already, there was a smell from the ambulance's other passenger, who had been killed by the initial impact. He looked at the nuns with newfound respect. "Are you really nuns, then?"

Sister Marie considered the unlikely accident and remarked. "What? You don't recognize an act of God when you see one?"

Then there was a shot. The driver had regained consciousness and inched his way to his silenced Luger. Before anyone could determine what had happened, Claude pivoted about and returned fire with his own Ruby pistol. "Put him back in the driver's seat. Everyone has to appear to have died in the accident."

Robespierre, however, continued to bark as if something still alarmed him. At first, no one paid him any mind, but then they followed his eyes, back to the maquisard.

Sister Beatrice looked at Claude and watched as his white neckerchief dyed itself crimson. She verbalized, what the others were still too stunned to express. "Claude dear...you've been shot."

Friedrich removed his dagger from the Bunsen burner. "There is a little game I like to play." He poured water on one side of the blade. "One side will burn you severely and the other side...only slightly-severely. Any time I don't like the answer to one of my questions, you feel the not-so-good side."

The doctor, held by two SS soldiers, was defiant, but appropriately scared. "I don't know anything. I am just a doctor."

Friedrich snickered. "There is no 'just' in war. The lowliest servant can forfeit a battle if he neglects his task. Now how did that patient manifest get changed?"

"I don't know."

The doctor's skin sizzled as the blade melted his cheek. "You'll have to do better than that. I find that people who have worthy answers are, rarely, so brief."

"It...it could have been anyone. There are many new people on staff." The doctor had anticipated that such an encounter was inevitable. He looked to his horrified peers, but they all turned away from him; afraid to share his misery.

Friedrich ran his thumb over the raised eagle insignia, on the handle of his dagger. "I think I should heat you again," he said, softly to it. "Don't you think?" He placed the blade over the burner and cranked up the heat; until the acid engraved motto 'Alles fur Deutschland,' glowed. "We found some nun habits near the garden. You wouldn't know anything about those, would you?"

Under the stress, the doctor was unable to hide his astonishment that they had been uncovered so quickly. It was not easy for him to predict the efficiency with which the Gestapo worked. "Obviously, the answer to all your questions. Local resistance disguised as nuns. I assure you...no one at the hospital was involved."

Friedrich removed the dagger from the flame and pressed it upon the doctor's neck. "Are you sure you aren't hiding something?"

Klaus who had been watching quietly, from a distance, interrupted. "They've found the ambulance on the road to Brassac. Are you nearly done?"

Friedrich searched himself for any, lingering, questions. "No, I was just about to make an example of him to help loosen his colleague's tongues."

"Very well then," replied Klaus. He pulled out his Luger and pointed it at the doctor. "Think of a number between one and ten."

"Five."

Klaus placed a bullet above the bridge of his nose and grabbed his coat. "Come Friedrich. I need you to drive me."

Disappointed, Friedrich turned to leave, but as they reached the door he asked, "Herr Klaus, what was the number? Don't tell me you didn't think of one, again?"

Klaus sucked a bit of air between his teeth. "You know Friedrich, I'm just not as good at these games as you are."

Claude was carried to where the roofs of Brassac peeked, ever so slightly, above the chestnut trees. Unable to continue through the pain, they laid him upon a pile of leaves. "Help me out of this habit. I'm not dying dressed like my mom."

Sister Anette removed the veil, serre-téte, cap, and his bloodstained neckerchief. She was unable to remove the habit skirt, due to his condition.

"We're almost there," Sister Marie encouraged him. "Just a little further."

Claude winced. "I only hung on to get you this far," he revealed. "You don't need me anymore."

"That's not true Claude," Sister Anette protested. "You must try! You must!"

200

He shook his head. "Apparently, somebody bigger than me is already looking out for you."

"Stop talking like that," Noele admonished. "You're not going to die. We're almost there!"

Claude attempted to laugh, but only coughed and fluid could be heard in his chest. "How are you ever going to be a nun if you lie like that?"

"You're a good man Claude," Sister Gabrielle observed. "Thank you."

"Thank you," repeated Anette and Beatrice.

Claude tried to say something sarcastic, but could only offer a half-smile. He put his hand on Robespierre, who pressed against his side and softly licked his hand. The dog whimpered and nuzzled him with his forehead.

"Don't be afraid Claude," Sister Marie comforted him. She spoke over Sister Beatrice, who had begun to perform his last rites. "There's nothing to be afraid of."

Claude's eyes glazed, and it appeared as if he was ready to succumb, but then he added, "I was...but then I met you--" With those words he stared into the trees and died.

Sister Beatrice finished and observed. "We will see you soon Claude. Put in a good word for us; God knows we'll need it."

Friedrich stopped the motorcycle at the charcoaled remains of the ambulance. Field-grey soldiers, busily, sifted through the wreckage and the terrible smell of burning flesh and rubber lingered. He now wondered if they had been in error, by trying to avoid the appearance of a military convoy.

One of the soldiers saw Klaus and rushed to greet him. "They got away, but they were unable to get the pilot out, and he burned to death in the back of the ambulance. I think you saw what they did further up the road?"

Klaus nodded and went to investigate the matter for himself. "And what of our driver and guard?"

"All dead, I'm afraid."

"I see." Klaus covered his mouth, with his handkerchief and peered into the back of the ambulance. Inside, a charred skeleton was still strapped to the gurney.

"Looks like they failed," offered the soldier.

Klaus gestured at the wreckage. "Does this look like failure? Du bist bekloppt!"

The soldier did not offer a defense for his opinion, but simply lowered his head and backed away.

"Herr Klaus!" cried Friedrich, from nearby. "Herr Klaus--"

"What Friedrich?" Klaus' patience was completely exhausted.

"There's something I think you should see."

Klaus walked to the front of the ambulance, where he found

Friedrich wearing an expression so twisted that it seemed a recreation of the scene. At first he did not see the source of Friedrich's attention, but then Klaus was able to deconstruct exactly what held his interest. "Friedrich, tell me that's not our car fused to the top of that ambulance."

Friedrich wondered whether his goal was to confirm his commander's worst suspicions or if hiding the truth was what he, actually, desired. "It would appear so."

"Why does somebody up there hate me?"

In Brassac's petite graveyard, they laid Claude to rest. His beret lay on his hands, and his face was covered with a handkerchief upon which they had drawn the Croix de Lorraine. The sisters watched over the fallen maquisard, from between the gravestones; like sepulchral angels.

"Normally, I'm called upon to say a few words," Father Jubé observed, "but in this case I think Sister Marie knew him better. I will only say that Claude moved me from indifference...to making a difference and for that I am grateful. He died so that others may live and do so freely."

Sister Marie put her hand on Father Jubé's shoulder. "Claude was not a religious man...unless he was talking about his gun. He did once ask me, though, why God allows death...why evil exists.

I told him that the real question, was not why such things exist, but what is our response? Claude was a living example of this idea. He was often an agent of death, but rarely have I seen someone so committed to preserving life. He was a stumbling block for evil and, therefore, an instrument of good. Rest sweetly, our friend and our brother."

CHAPTER FOURTEEN
THE MOUNT OF OLIVES

The cafe was still called Chez Honoré and it appeared, more or less, the same with its quaint tables and colorful umbrellas. René's lunch, however, was reminiscent of something an army mess hall might reject. One might attribute that to its new chef, a gruff Germanic-looking fellow, who appeared to have been recently re-assigned from the front lines. The company who sat across from the mayor was, equally, disagreeable. Klaus was in a most foul mood. Unable to drown him out through the pleasure of his meal, René was forced to drink of the German's bitterness.

Klaus was blunt. "I'm going to be direct with you. I can't prove it yet, but I think your local clergy is involved with the resistance."

René objected, at once. "No, don't be absurd. They have no interest in politics." He waved his fork for dramatic effect.

"And why should you have such an interest in their welfare?" Klaus took a sip of the wine he had brought.

"Well," began René, "they are essential to the stability of this community. Look at the damage done by what happened to this cafe...not that you weren't justified in the matter, but look! I've lost three kilograms!"

Klaus smiled for the first time. "It is pretty bad. I had

Friedrich select the chef, but his tastes are as bland as his personality."

René saw something that turned his stomach even more than the food. Chloé sat at a nearby table, enjoying lunch with a German officer. He had heard the rumours, but did not like being forced to suffer the physical confirmation. Her outfit did not fool him, as he recognized the cloth from other ensembles. "I'd like to ease your mind on this matter. As mayor, I will look into it personally. Please leave everything to me."

Klaus was not about to forego his own investigation, but neither was he about to turn down additional help. "Do you know how I got this post?" He tried to carve his steak, but it resisted his efforts. "In the summer of '34 the president of Catholic Action gave a speech in Berlin. I led the group that shot him in his office and sent his staff to concentration camps." He smiled as his knife finally passed through the tendon. "He had outlived his usefulness. I suspect that the clergy here has, likewise, outlived their usefulness. Please see that you do not, also."

"Maybe we can get him out by rail," suggested Sister Beatrice.

Sister Marie shook her head. "We're the ones who took that card off the table."

"What?" asked Sister Dominique. "Blowing up bridges is fun--"

"What happened to the safe house in Moissac and a plane pickup from a field?" wondered Sister Beatrice.

Marie thought about it for a minute. "Yes, well, I'm afraid that's no longer safe. Michel says the area is locked up pretty tight, after what happened at the hospital. As for a pickup, we still don't have the right radio equipment."

The pilot walked in drinking a cup of tea Noele had made him. "Still trying to get me out of here? Am I that offensive?"

"What? Don't you want to go home? All that lovely British cuisine to look forward to?" It was an unusually saucy observation for Sister Beatrice.

He looked at her cross. "Oh, like snails are a culinary gift for the ages." They shared a disgusted look, but then both laughed. "Yes, I want to go home; the tea here is terrible. Now if only you could steal me a plane--"

The sisters sat in silence and contemplated their dilemma.

"Maybe that's not such a bad idea?" Sister Marie rose to allow the blood to flow to all the right organs. "That's what Claude would have done...the obvious, but unexpected."

"Now wait a minute," interjected the pilot. "I'd have to fly that Nazi bird into Allied territory. Getting shot down by your mates can be embarrassing."

"But could you fly a German plane?" pressed Beatrice. "You could go to Italy and make your way back to England."

"Sure...especially if I don't have to use it again. That said, when you log more crashes than landings, it's time to hang your wings up." The pilot was a bit offended that his abilities were being held in doubt. "The question is not can I fly it, but can you get me into a cockpit."

Now it was the sister's opportunity to be wounded. "We got you out of the hospital didn't we?" asked Sister Gabrielle.

"As I recall, you had help," corrected the pilot. He looked around, but nobody disagreed.

Sister Dominique pulled a rope with Robespierre. "Didn't we talk about hitting an airbase?"

"I thought you said bouillabaisse," objected Sister Anette. "Guess I'll be getting my ears checked."

The pilot made a face, not at all impressed with the French interpretation of afternoon tea. "An airbase...Vicky would like that idea, very much."

"Your girlfriend?" asked Noele.

The pilot laughed. "No...far more serious, I'm afraid. She was my plane."

The chair challenged René to find any faults. Though it was

his desire to deliver it to Father Jubé immediately, Sister Marie had insisted that they wait until Sunday so that it could be presented before the entire town. The chair was a fitting expression of the community's gratitude for the priest's years of service, but more than that, it had become a metaphor of its creator's reformation. It was a physical admonition to transcend mere practicality. Knowing its intended recipient was on his way, he covered it with a wool blanket.

The mayor heard a knock at the door, but it was not unexpected. "Father, thank you for coming? Did anyone follow you?"

"No, I followed your instructions to the letter. Why so late René?"

"There's something critical I need to tell you."

Father Jubé seemed to understand the gravity of the news he was about to receive. He looked for a place to sit and almost chose the covered chair, but then decided to continue to stand. "Yes, do go on--"

"I could be imprisoned or even killed for what I'm about to tell you."

"Then, by all means, don't tell me!" He held his fingers across his lips and paced. "René, I'd rather not put you at risk." It was intentional that they had never discussed his involvement in the resistance. Father Jubé knew that René had to fulfill his role in dealing with the Germans while doing his best to keep them at arm's length. Deniability had to be maintained, for the safety of all parties. "My well-being is secondary to that of my students. There's no need to inform me."

René, however, had reached a point where he needed to expand his purpose. "I'm a grown man now...I'm the mayor of Brassac. More than that, I could not live with myself if I didn't."

"I won't hear you." Father Jubé headed for the door though he knew that such a breach in protocol must indicate an emergency. Still, he did not wish to be a party to it.

"It's about Sister Marie."

Father Jubé froze in place, and his protests stilled. He sat on the corner of the desk and forced his mouth to speak the words his conscious protested. "Alright René...I'm listening."

Léon entered the back door, which led into the nun's kitchen. He hit his head on one of the copper pots, which was older than the nuns themselves, and was surprised to find himself alone with Noele. Her presence stirred affections that would soon, no doubt, be the cause of an uncomfortable confessional visit. "Oh, sorry...I was just looking for Father Jubé. He doesn't seem to be around." He began to perspire, although it was quite cold outside. "Well, I'll try the Sacristy again."

"Léon...wait," Noele requested. "There's something I've wanted to share with you. Have a seat. Please?"

Léon pulled up the stool that René had repaired. He wasn't aware of the craftsman, but he took a moment to appreciate how unusually well balanced and comfortable it was. "How is the pilot doing?"

"Good, I think. He speaks a little French, but Sister Marie and Sister Beatrice speak better English than I do."

"That's nice. Where are the others?" He looked around nervously. "Are they coming back soon?"

Noele brought out two mugs and gave him one. "Go ahead. Try it."

He took a sip and his eyes, immediately, widened. It was a taste, unlike anything he had experienced in a great while.

"It's the coffee you brought me. Every time I drink it I think about how kind your were to remember."

"It was nothing." He was too self-effacing to take a compliment or any due credit.

"Don't be so modest. I know you must have risked getting shot for this, no? Would even a bottle of Chambertin from Napoleon's cellar be as precious?"

Léon pretended that it was nothing. "It's just coffee--" He tried his best, not to make eye-contact with her.

She smiled and lifted his chin. "Exactly. You gave me a piece of my life back. I don't think anyone has ever done something so kind for me. Thank you."

Léon could not understand why René would flee to Paris at the thought of a lifetime of such complete and utter happiness. He didn't know how to respond to such a sentiment, so he tried to change the subject. "What will you do after the war?"

"After the war?"

"I don't think it can last forever." Léon wasn't sure, however if that was true.

"I'm not sure. When I drink this...this amazing coffee, I remember things--"

"Like what?" Léon hardly ever thought about the day before and certainly not the one to come.

She took a sip and stared off into a place far within her memories. "People and places that meant everything, but are now lost. The person I was before those things became memories."

Léon was too straightforward to get involved in such a philosophical conversation. Even then, he could tell that the coffee had become more than a mere beverage in the excavation of her psyche. "But, you still want to become a nun, right?" It occurred to him that the question might not be appropriate.

Noele drew her mouth, into a thought. "Maybe, if I can forget myself, again." She finished her cup. "This is really great coffee."

Léon knew what she revealed was important, but he struggled to comprehend her meaning.

"And if my previous life won't have me."

"This is where we used to ride our bikes. You were so handsome. What happened?" Sister Marie teased, as they walked the small country trail that led north from Brassac. Light peeked through the branches of the trees, and everything appeared the same as it had been; in times of peace.

"Yes, I was much better looking back then," Father Jubé laughed, "but you haven't changed."

Sister Marie blushed. "There aren't enough 'Our Fathers' for a lie like that," then she turned to him and grinned, "but don't stop telling them!"

He discovered that she had coaxed a smile out of him. "Ok, but if I don't get to Heaven...it'll be on your head." They walked for a few more minutes, content simply to enjoy each other's company. He had brought her, away from the town, for a more serious purpose. Now, though, it seemed too wonderful a day to spoil. He realized that his reasons for holding back, were selfish and that he had to let her know the true state of their condition. "Marie--"

"Yes?"

"There's something I need to warn you about."

She looked into his eyes and saw that they shook from distress. "What is it? Francis, what's wrong?"

"The Germans suspect that you've been aiding the resistance. Soon they will come for you. They're, no doubt just planning the most opportune time. They know how popular you are in the community, but that is only a matter of logistics."

Marie had hoped that such a day could be postponed until the end of the war, but never did she believe that such a time could be entirely avoided. "And what of the other sisters?"

"They will probably arrest you first and then determine who else was responsible. They will get you to talk by any means necessary. Marie, you must not allow them to take you."

"I see," she replied.

It was not the answer, however, that he sought. He knew that those were the words she defaulted to when she wished not to agree. "You have to flee, immediately. I can have Léon take you out from here today. Just tell me which personal belongings you'd like us to collect, and we will meet you here tonight."

Marie thought quietly until the outcome of her thoughts could only be held in doubt. Then she replied, "No...if I hide they would surely take the others. My feet stand upon the Mount of Olives. It has to be me."

He refused to hear her conclusion. "There has to be another way. I just need time to think. Wait here and let me go talk with the others. Please...just give me an hour."

Sister Marie agreed, but only with her eyes. She watched as Father Jubé ran towards the town, with the same enthusiasm as when she had known him as Francis, the boy who had taught her everything about what it meant to love.

"I can round them up tonight," Friedrich protested. "It needs to be done quickly before they have time to hide anything."

Klaus had already made up his mind, but he was still engaged in the intellectual exercise of allowing Friedrich to convince him. This allowed the matter to be weighed from a variety of angles, that he might not have considered. "On one hand, rounding up the clergy will make things more difficult to manage for a while. Then again, Martin Bormann himself has said that the very security of the Reich rests on ending church influence."

"Well, there you go," replied Friedrich. "Where's my dagger?"

Klaus held up his hand to pause his enthusiasm. "Then again, the Füerer wishes that we are pragmatic with regards to the church, until such time as we can eliminate them entirely."

Friedrich looked confused. "Does that mean I'm going...or

not?"

There was the rustling of things within his desk and then Klaus threw Friedrich some keys.

"Another car?"

"Yes, it's just another Kübelwagen, but marginally better than the side-car." He returned to the document that he was signing. "And don't lose this one."

Klaus was relieved not to have to drive the motorcycle. "Excellent. What are my orders?"

"Just the mother superior, for now. Once we have all the information we need, we'll be able to determine how many others need to be brought in. The town is restless enough over the incident with the chef, so we'll have to use a little discretion."

"That's really not my strong suit," Friedrich replied.

A couple hours passed, yet Sister Marie had still not returned. The sisters read, worked on needlework and tried to keep busy to pass the time. Robespierre sat on the floor moping, in apparent sympathy with the general mood of the room. Then there was a knock at the door, and they opened it to discover death positioned within its frame.

Friedrich did not bother with any of the pleasantries of social decorum. He was accompanied by four SS officers and wore a long, leather coat that was wet from the rain. The nuns gazed up, from their drudgery, and stared in disbelief that the moment they had dreaded had finally arrived. He considered the indifference with which he was received, but failed to recognize that it was a posture that had been previously agreed upon. "Good evening, sisters. Is your mother superior here?"

Sister Beatrice stood erect and replied, "She is currently out. Is there something we can tell her for you?"

It was not the answer he had expected. "I see, well, I can not simply return empty-handed. There are some serious questions that need to be addressed." Friedrich would rather have taken the lot of them in and considered, for a moment, that this might be his chance to modify Klaus' instructions.

"It's me you're looking for," replied Father Jubé, who had appeared at the door. His hair soaked; he panted like he had run a great distance to embrace the moment.

Friedrich knew of the priest, but was still surprised at the direction his investigation had taken. "And why should I be looking for you?"

Father Jubé stuck out his hand, which held a brick of plastic explosives. "I'm the one helping the resistance. The nuns know nothing about it, and I can prove it to you."

The Nazi's eyes lit up. "Really? Your honesty is most

refreshing, but I am afraid we will have to examine your sincerity...most thoroughly."

Father Jubé took the Germans to his office and showed them the space behind the bookcase. It still held weapons and most of the ammunition he had stockpiled. What interested Friedrich the most, however, were the clergy vestments stacked in one corner.

"I shared these with the local resistance. I alone am responsible for these actions," the priest explained.

"And who was your contact?" Friedrich demanded.

Father Jubé led him to the cemetery and pointed at Claude's freshly-dug grave. "If you dig you will find that he was buried with his Basque beret and the flag of the resistance. With him died everything I know."

"Of that we shall see," replied Friedrich, who motioned for the priest to be restrained. "Place him in my car. I am taking him into custody. Rest assured, soon we will all get what we want. I will get the truth and you...martyrdom."

Sister Marie waited until her patience was overcome by her concern. She ran to the nunnery and threw the door open to find the other sisters huddled together, sobbing. "Where is he?" she asked. "Where's Francis?"

Sister Beatrice tried to embrace her and communicate what she could not put into words. Sister Marie refused to listen and pushed her aside. "No! Where is he? Where's Father Jubé?" She ran inside the church, screaming his name; unwilling to accept a reality without the only man she had ever loved. Unable to accept that she remained because he had taken her place.

Marie flew through the streets of Brassac, crying his name, hysterically. Finally, she stumbled upon René's workshop. The door was cracked open, and an amber light shone from the candles he had lit. She peered inside and saw he was on his knees and clutched the chair that he had finally finished. He had buried his face in its velvet seat and made a sound like a wounded animal, as he rocked back and forth. Seeing the man who was like a son to Father Jubé, beyond consolation, she understood that denial would no longer be her willing partner. She looked upon the crown of the chair and saw that René had carved a quote Father Jubé had taught him as a boy, "The student is not above the teacher." Marie collapsed upon her knees and wept.

CHAPTER FIFTEEN
ART, NOT FURNITURE

Sister Dominique tapped lightly on the floor. "You can come out now."

One of the wood planks lifted and the pilot's head popped out. "I had started to think that I'd been forgotten." It was, unfortunately, true.

The nuns had cried to the point of dehydration and now sat, red-eyed, and still. Sister Marie had assumed a crumpled and withdrawn position on her bed. No one dared intervene. Words could only agitate what time would heal.

There was a knock and Léon let himself in. "I'm sorry to disturb you." The room seemed an unwelcome place in which to venture. A somber air hung about, like smoke in a room with a closed flue.

Noele appeared beside him and whispered, "Léon, it's not the right time. Return tomorrow, no?"

He seemed, honestly, to consider her request, but then replied. "I can't. Father Jubé insisted that I read this letter, immediately after he was arrested."

Everyone took notice and even Sister Marie, sat up to hear what he had to say.

"I'll just read it then," he concluded. "To whom it may concern." He paused to explain, "He didn't want it to point to you if the message was intercepted." Nobody seemed to appreciate his commentary, so he continued. "Please do not despair at my arrest. The course of events has not been dictated by our enemies, but determined by providence. It remains, however, for you to bring this plan to fruition, by ensuring that our wounded bird makes it back across the pond--"

"He means the pilot," interrupted Sister Anette.

"Nothing gets by you," observed Sister Gabrielle.

Léon continued, "and the French vine that has withered, is redeemed."

"What is that supposed to mean? Besides, we don't have our gear," protested Sister Dominique.

"I hid the best of the weapons in an unmarked grave. The gentleman who is reading this letter--"

"Did he just call Léon a gentleman?" asked Beatrice.

"The gentleman," Léon repeated for effect, "will help you retrieve them...assuming he buried everything as instructed." He paused to verify, "Which I did." He ran his index finger up and down the note, to find where he had left off. "Lastly, I have enclosed the time and place where you will rendezvous with your new contact. I asked the esteemed gentleman reading this--"

"Did he, actually, just say esteemed gentleman?" asked Sister

Gabrielle.

"Esteemed gentleman," Léon repeated, "to be my replacement, but to his credit he was too humble."

"Let me see that," demanded Sister Gabrielle.

Léon ignored her and continued, "Being firm in your faith, you must not despair, but persevere in all things; for quitting is the sacrament of failure."

The message having concluded, Sister Marie rolled over and withdrew like a woodlouse. She knew that those would be the last words she would ever hear from him.

In the drawing room of his manor, Klaus drank brandy and enjoyed a roaring fire of cedar wood. "Well, it would appear that we have settled the matter of the resistance, just in time for General Eckart's arrival."

"Perhaps," Friedrich replied. "I still think we should have brought in all of the nuns."

"Friedrich. Friedrich. The nuns aren't going anywhere. They're convinced they have a reprieve, which will keep things quiet during the general's visit; which is all I really care about. Then you can press the matter further if necessary."

It was true that Klaus had an acumen for political reasoning that both impressed and perplexed Friedrich. "But what about getting to the truth?"

Klaus guffawed. "In a bureaucracy, appearance is far more important than truth." He poured himself another dram of whiskey. "Did you finally finish with the priest?"

"It's all done, but he didn't have any further information."

This struck Klaus as rather peculiar. "Did you try the heretic's fork? Might have been a poetic touch...him being a priest and all."

Friedrich was almost insulted. "Of course. I did everything short of draw and quarter him."

"Well, after the last time with the tanks--"

The stunt had nearly gotten Friedrich reassigned until Klaus had intervened. "Yes, well, he was still in one piece when I put him on the train to the Pfarreblock, but I doubt he'll survive long."

"You know," said Klaus, who swirled his brandy. "I was considered for the job at the Drancy Internment Camp."

Friedrich looked up surprised. Klaus had never mentioned any such aspirations.

"...but Alois Brunner got it instead." It was the story of Klaus' career.

"Well," consoled Friedrich, "it's probably for the best...the guards there are all French."

"I hear you're not eating."

René looked up to find Noele standing at the doorway, holding a black kettle. "I'm not hungry." Steam rose from the pot, and a memorable smell reached his nose. "Is that--"

Noele nodded. "Yes, it's soupe aux chataignes--"

"Well...maybe just a bite." René had not had her chestnut soup since before he withdrew to Paris. He had assumed he would never taste it again, after the events that had transpired between them. They had not even had a proper talk since he had returned, and most of their interactions could best be described as confrontational or awkward.

"Well," Noele sighed, glad to see that he was enjoying it. "I'd better go--"

The soup smelled like honey, and he realized that she must have peeled all of the chestnuts herself. For a soup favored by the poor the flavor was luxurious, like velvet, and even better than he remembered. René had tried to find its replacement in Paris, but without success. "Could you please stay for a bit?" He looked like he hadn't slept.

She sat beside him, nervously looking for a topic of conversation. "Your chair came out beautifully."

"Je te remercie."

"I know Father Jubé meant a lot to you." Noele wanted to help him, but their relationship had regressed back to mere pleasantries. "You never knew your real father, did you?" Now she wondered if she was only making matters worse. The other nuns made ministering seem so easy.

René looked at her, utterly wounded; as if he hoped she would end his misery. A hunger strike was out of the question, though, as the soup had successfully restored his appetite.

"I stopped eating after you left," she revealed. "Sister Marie would have none of that, though--" Noele wondered how long they would dance around the subject that had created a chasm between them.

René's spoon scraped the bottom of the kettle. "I'm sorry."

"What?" She had longed dreamed of hearing the words, but never expected they would be spoken; except in her imagination.

"For hurting you." He waited to see if she would absolve him. Her veil and habit made such a thing appear possible.

Noele smiled. "If you didn't want to get married you should have just said so."

"I know. I'm sorry. I was...so stupid."

She took the pot from him and whispered. "Good."

"This is where Claude showed me how to pick a lock." The other nuns glared at Sister Anette. "What? I've already used it twice back home."

"Well, maybe you should stop losing the keys," snapped Sister

Gabrielle.

Their camp appeared forlorn without the maquisard's, impatient instructions and Father Jubé's tolerant advice. It seemed to suffer from neglect though nothing physically had changed.

"How long should we stay?" asked Sister Beatrice.

"Whatever seems best," replied Sister Marie, indifferently. She sat in the corner, more than willing to let others assume the mantel of leadership.

"We need to be home in time for Vespers...and I don't need a new contact, anyway." Sister Dominique, was not the only one who was resistant to starting anew.

"Alright," agreed Sister Marie. "Let's head home."

"Bonjour," heralded a raspy voice. They turned and saw Philippe, uncharacteristically sober, with a rifle slung over his shoulder.

Robespierre pulled against his leash and growled.

"We're caught!" cried Sister Beatrice. She instinctively reached for her riffle, but Léon had yet to deliver their weapons.

Sister Marie looked up, indifferently. "Do whatever you want Philippe...we won't resist."

Philippe grinned and stomped out the cigarette that had been dangling from his mouth. "I'm not here to arrest you...I'm here to join you!"

"What--" exclaimed Sister Beatrice. "What did he just say?"

"He's a collaborator," cried Sister Gabrielle. "He's trying to set us up!"

Philippe reached into his shirt and pulled out a note, which he handed to Marie.

Marie read it while the others kept a close eye on Philippe, whose association with the Germans was well established.

"What is it?" asked Sister Noele. "What does it say?" She looked over her shoulder and tried to read.

Sister Marie finished and handed it back to Philippe. "It's from Father Jubé. René came to him, on Philipe's behalf, with the intent to help him restore his reputation. This happened just before Francis gave himself up for arrest."

Philippe tore the note into pieces and began to chew the message like tobacco. He could see, however, that the nuns were appalled by the request. "Well...do you believe in redemption or don't you?"

Sister Gabrielle was the first to move. She walked up to Philippe and handed him something wrapped in a handkerchief.

"What is this?" asked Philippe. Inside he discovered a well-used handgun.

"It was Claude's...but it's yours now. Deserve it or die trying."

"This is the honorable mayor of Brassac," Klaus explained, as he introduced René to General Eckart. They sat outside Chez Honoré, enjoying a cheese plate and the afternoon light.

"Come and have a drink with us," replied the general. "Klaus tells me that German wine is your favorite."

"Does he?" replied René, quizzically. "What brings you to our humble corner of France?"

Klaus saw the room in René's glass as a challenge, so he filled it with more wine. "The general is here to see that things are running like a Bavarian clock."

"A challenge, considering the place is teaming with French," the general laughed, uproariously.

René failed to see the humor, but sipped the wine and tried not to make a face. *A cuckoo clock*, he thought to himself.

"Perhaps the mayor would like to join us for dinner?"

"Um...yes. Absolutely." René was caught off-guard. "I'd be delighted. How long will you be with us?"

"I fly back to Berlin tomorrow. It would seem reports of things not being well at hand, were a bit exaggerated."

"I have many enemies," protested Klaus. "One must not believe everything they hear within the halls of pencil pushers."

The mayor attempted to sympathize. "In politics, your effectiveness is best measured by the outrage of your enemies."

"Well said," replied the general. "Say, Klaus. Why haven't you mentioned that you enjoy such sage local support? I'm starting to think I might have uncovered the reason for your success?"

Klaus dabbed his mouth, with his napkin, and tried not to appear annoyed.

"I have received word from the mayor that a visiting general will be flying out of Toulouse-Montaudran," reported Philippe.

The pilot was intrigued. "Any idea what he arrived in?"

"Yes, apparently it was a Junkers Ju 52. It's being repaired while he's here. Can you fly it?" Philippe took the pilot's hostile glare as affirmation and did not pursue additional verification.

"Are we sure the information is reliable?" asked Sister Gabrielle.

"The mayor had dinner with him, just last night. The airfield is attached to a factory the general visited. I went early this morning and verified the information."

"Who are you?" asked Sister Noele. It was true that Philippe was an entirely different man, sober.

"Is it defended?" asked Sister Beatrice.

"There aren't any actual defenses, but it's also a base for training replacement units."

"And that's bad?" asked Sister Anette.

Sister Gabrielle palmed her face.

"So we'll have no problem getting on the field," Sister Marie concluded, "but little hope of getting off of it?"

"That would appear to be the case," Philippe confirmed. "Please decide soon, we have to act by morning."

"It's not enough time," complained the pilot. "We'll have to think of something else. It's not the only plane--"

Sister Marie's interest in the future had diminished. "Our objective is to get you home...not us."

Under a strawberry moon, Léon dug into the soil beside Claude's grave. His shovel hit the box that hid the few weapons he had been able to secure, the night that Father Jubé was arrested. "Don't worry Claude," he whispered. "I will not disturb you."

"We're counting on you," Sister Marie informed Léon. "Remember, everything must be on the plane when we arrive."

Léon gulped and his Adam's apple bounced as if upon a trampoline. It was nothing like lifting pastries. He had no idea what he would discover when he got to the airbase.

Sister Marie put her arm on Léon's shoulder. "You have one hour until we join you. The general is scheduled to leave at six a.m. Good luck."

"Don't worry," protested Noele. "Léon will have everything ready." She handed him a small bag with some tools and a piece of cheese. "Do you have a way to get there?"

"Yes, I stole a motorcycle," he replied. "It's quite nice. It even has a sidecar."

"And how are we getting there?" asked the pilot.

"Mule cart," Marie informed him. "So we'd better leave now."

Friedrich hated to wake up early, but the task, of driving the General to the airport, was his lot. There was no way Klaus could be bothered to get out of bed, at such an hour. The Kübelwagen resisted starting, when he twisted the key. Friedrich's breath looked like spider webs, from the morning chill.

"Is there a problem?" asked the general.

"We've had some transportation issues. We had a motorcycle, but it seems to have gone missing."

The general thought about this, then offered. "Maybe I can find something more appropriate when I get back to Berlin?"

"Thank you sir," said Friedrich who gunned the engine as it roared to life, but he had learned not to get his hopes up.

Léon snuck into the aircraft hangar, through an open door, and did his best to search without turning on the lights. His shoulder caught something on the edge of a table and steel bearings bounced across the cement floor. He cringed and waited to see if he had attracted anyone's attention.

Everything remained still, so he let himself into the building that was adjoined to it. Fortunately it appeared far more promising, as it was stuffed with pilot supplies; such as uniforms, headphones, and stacks of already packed parachutes. Léon dressed in one of the Luftwaffe uniforms he found, but it hung comically on his slight frame.

Suddenly, the door creaked open and in walked an actual pilot. He looked like he had just stepped out of a Nazi recruiting poster, in his well-pressed uniform. "Guten Morgen," they casually exclaimed.

Léon grunted and pretended to look through a logbook he had found, knowing as much about German as flying.

"Wohin heute?" asked the pilot.

Léon just smiled back.

"Wohin heute?" he asked, louder.

Léon kept smiling, but it was clear that something was amiss. Seeing his friendly demeanor change, Léon took the initiative and threw his best sucker punch. The pilot caught it in his fist and let out an amused laugh. He returned a jab that sent Léon flying back into the pile of parachutes. Now he assumed a rather stiff fighting posture, as he crossed towards him.

Léon grabbed an unpacked parachute, and threw its canopy

over him. The Luftwaffe pilot became entangled as he struggled against the suspension lines. Léon found a small shovel and swung where his head appeared to be. The parachute collapsed, but there wasn't time to hide the German pilot. After he had searched his pockets for keys, he just wrapped him; like a spider might a fly.

Friedrich entered the room, bleary-eyed, and looking quite short of sleep. "Good, our pilot is here. Is the plane ready?" he asked in German.

Léon just held his thumb up, in an ambiguous, but positive gesture. He was very skilled at appearing to look busy.

Friedrich attributed the gesture his own meaning and replied, "All right, then. Just let me know when we're ready." He went outside to help the general with his bags. "The pilot is going to be a few minutes. Preparations and such."

"Well, tell him to be quick, it's blasted cold," the general complained.

They watched as Léon came out, overloaded with parachutes that he stuffed into the Ju 52.

"Are you sure this plane is safe?" asked the general.

"I was assured that all the repairs have been made," he replied.

Again, Léon went in and returned carrying three more parachutes.

"He's a very cautious pilot," Friedrich observed.

Philippe pulled on the reins and brought the wagon to a halt. "Someone is already there." The airfield was partially lit, and he could see shadows scurry about within the fog. "It might already be the general."

Sister Dominique grabbed her bow. "Léon is in there. I thought they weren't supposed to be here yet?"

"Stick to the plan," instructed Sister Marie. "Divvy up the explosives."

As they crept closer, they could see lights were on in one of the buildings, and two figures hovered near the plane.

"The timing is no good," protested the RAF pilot. "I think it's an abort."

"We've seen worse," replied Sister Marie. "Teams of two to a plane. Three-minute fuses. You know the rest."

Sister Dominique took her aside. "You're not trying to rush your reunion with Francis, are you?"

"Just follow the plan," she ordered.

The sisters divided into pairs and crawled through the tall grass, each selecting a plane to which they attached one of the plastic explosives; Leon had acquired for them.

"Tell them they can come out now," bellowed a voice behind them. It had a Franconian accent and attached to its hand was a Luger.

"No," Sister Marie replied, and turned away. She did not,

particularly, care if she was shot.

"Tell them to drop their guns," Friedrich demanded and grabbed her. He pressed his pistol hard enough against her temple, that it indented her skin.

Sister Beatrice was not as indifferent. "Everyone come out!" she cried.

Friedrich appreciated the change of attitude. "How fortunate that we should meet under such circumstances. I've been looking forward to this for some time."

"Funny, my rifle said the same thing." Sister Marie was not intimidated by his threats.

Sisters Beatrice, Gabrielle, Annette, and Noele appeared with their hands up. Sister Dominique threw her bow upon the pile.

"Finally, all my questions are answered. You are the nuns from Brassac, are you not? That priest lied to me! What is the world coming to? If only Klaus had let me use the tanks."

The general came over and addressed his sidearm at them. "Well, this is impressive, Friedrich! Was this little display planned for me?"

Friedrich did not miss a beat. "Jawhl! As you can see, the resistance has been dealt with. Herr Klaus has been teaching me about fishing."

General Eckart was both surprised and impressed. "And you used me to draw them out? Clearly I have not given you, or your commander, sufficient credit."

Sister Marie was despondent at the thought that she had led them into such a rudimentary trap. Claude, she felt, would never have made such a mistake. The entirety of her being felt insufficient and defeated.

I've already called for help," the general informed them. "It is no problem to wait until we see them off."

Léon watched from within the plane and pretended to go through his pre-flight. He searched around the cockpit for a weapon, but found nothing more useful than a flashlight.

I picked a bad time to quit drinking, thought Philippe, as he watched their plan fall apart.

"What do we do now?" asked the British pilot.

"Stay here," Philippe instructed. "Something just occurred to me." He chambered a round, in his rifle and walked casually into the standoff.

Philippe?" wondered Friedrich. "You're all they sent?"

"Don't worry," Philippe replied. "I'm enough," and with that he shot the general. "Oh, and I resign."

"Well, aren't you a disappointment," Friedrich replied. "Nothing here has changed. I'm walking out of here, and I think she'll be coming with me this time." He led Sister Marie to the plane and yelled, "Start the engines. We're leaving."

Léon stared back bewildered and not sure how to respond.

"What? Is the Luftwaffe admitting imbeciles now?" Friedrich smacked him on his head to prompt a reaction. "The general is dead. Take me to the next airfield, just get us out of here!"

The nuns collected their weapons and moved towards the door of the plane. From inside, Sister Marie admonished them. "Stay where you are! Don't risk anything for me." Friedrich smiled at them as he latched the door.

"We don't have much time. He's going to figure out Léon can't fly." Philippe chambered a bullet in Claude's gun. "We'll have to do something."

"We're open to ideas," replied Sister Gabrielle.

"Don't you see? She has to want to live," Sister Beatrice explained. "If she can't imagine a life without Francis...she just won't fight."

Inside the airplane, Friedrich was becoming increasingly agitated. Léon was doing his best to pretend he was busy, but Friedrich was an expert in determining when the appearance of a situation felt wrong. It was difficult to both hold his pistol at Sister Marie and ascertain Léon's credentials as an aviator. Marie noticed that Friedrich preoccupied Léon, enough, that she could move to the side of where his barrel pointed. She grabbed Friedrich's arm, but he was able to fire; blowing a small hole in the skin of the plane. Marie's ears rang, but she could hear Friedrich gagging as Léon took the cord from his headset and wrapped it around his neck. The gun flew to the rear of the plane, but he kicked Sister Marie in the jaw. She saw flashes, but grabbed his dagger as he struggled with Léon.

"Where's Father Jubé?" she screamed. "And I'd better like the answer!"

"In a concentration camp," he gasped.

"Wrong answer, she replied and threw it at his chest. "Start telling me what I want to hear!"

Friedrich coughed, and blood spilled from his mouth. "Killing me won't change anything and I can see that I've already cut you deeper."

His scarlet smile made her wonder if he hoped she would finish the job. Perhaps, in his twisted world, getting her to stoop to his level would represent a perverse form of redemption. She unlatched the door to the plane, but Friedrich pulled the dagger from his chest and prepared to drive it into her. Philippe, however, slipped Claude's pistol through the opening and brought a conclusion to the arc of their association.

"Are you ok?" asked Philippe. "Can we toss him outside and get the hell out of here?"

"Yes, Philippe. Kindly do so." Her face was ruddy from the mist of his last shot.

The rest of the nuns climbed aboard, doing their best to ignore what Friedrich's demise had done to the interior of the plane.

"Looking for a real pilot?" joked the RAF airman, as he entered the cockpit.

Sister Marie smiled back and asked, "What is your name, anyway?"

"Osmond, but don't get too attached. I have to fly this thing to Italy. Too bad I'd never make it over the Channel."

"We've got to go!" cried Léon, looking out the front window. He could see several Wehrmacht soldiers hovering over the general's body. Klaus had arrived and gestured urgently at the plane.

The British pilot smiled. "Right. Best hurry...I lit the fuses."

"You what?" asked Philippe.

"No time to explain. Time to go," the pilot replied. He started the Ju 52's engines and immediately began to taxi. "Bloody hard on the engines, but...no choice."

Klaus and the soldiers ran towards the plane, but as they did a Dornier Do-17 exploded, and rained shards of aluminum down upon them. Then, a pair of Dewoitine D.520s blew apart, and the shockwaves knocked them from their feet.

"Can we go yet?" asked Sister Marie.

"I'm not familiar with this plane. Do I need flaps? I don't bloody know," he replied, as he took the runway. "Hold on and if you're really nuns, best start praying."

The plane seemed to accelerate slowly and then lifted into a shallow, lumbering climb.

"We're a bit heavy," complained the pilot, as the airfield shrank behind them. Léon, Philippe, and the sisters strapped on their parachutes not confident in what they were about to do, but even less convinced of the alternative. They sat, quietly, and gathered their courage for their final act of heroism.

"Are we near Mazamet?" asked Philippe.

"Just north," replied the pilot.

Philippe's face radiated an optimistic sheen. "Maybe, I'll go find my wife?" He smiled, knowingly, at Sister Marie and jumped from the plane. They ran to the door and watched his parachute open. He drifted away beneath them, leaving no doubt that while the war continued, he had found peace.

"We're almost to Brassac," the pilot informed them, "but I don't think it'll be safe for a while."

"We'll jump near Lamontélarié," Sister Marie replied.

"Wouldn't you like me to take you a bit further?"

"Not on your life," replied Sister Dominique. "We have to go back and get Robespierre."

Sister Marie checked the other's parachutes, though she was no expert herself. Claude had once practiced with them, by demonstrating how to jump from the top of some old crates. At the time, it seemed ridiculous to imagine that they would have a genuine opportunity to utilize such a skill.

"I can't do it," Sister Anette stammered. She stood by the open door, paralyzed with fear.

"No place worth jumping to is ever certain," Sister Marie consoled her. "We can all choose to stay safe, where we are, but isn't it more exciting to jump?" Then she pushed Anette, who screamed bloody murder, as she fell from the plane. "And sometimes...we have to be pushed."

Sister Anette was not alone for long, as the rest of the sisters jumped swiftly behind her. They hung, suspended, together in a place betwixt heaven and war. Above the howl of the wind, could be heard their singing and cries of joy. For though uncertain about what lay below, they were secure in the knowledge that the truth could never be defeated. Through their individual acts of resistance, they had transcended indifference and become living works of art.

EPILOGUE
RECONCILIATION AND JUSTICE

After the Normandy invasion, the sisters returned to Brassac; having spent over a year under the care of a church in Grenoble. Unable to follow their host's instructions to remain sequestered, they helped further its reputation as the Capital of the Maquis.

In Brassac, upon word of the liberation of France, many of the townspeople gathered collaborators into the streets; as occurred throughout the country. René came out of his workshop to find Chloé, on her knees, about to have her head shaved by several of the townspeople. Seeing René, and knowing the pain he had endured as she entertained the German officers, one of them handed him a pair of shears. René held them for a moment, but then cast them to the ground.

"She's a horizontal collaborator!" cried one of the men. The party moved forward to help settle the matter, but René pulled his pistol and fired into the air.

"I see a crowd of vertical ones...if you ask me," he replied. "This one will be keeping her hair, thank you very much."

Then the mob grew still, and René wondered why their faces mirrored such astonishment. He turned to discover Chloé, the shears in her hands. She, willfully, cut her own hair, and her sodden eyes looked deeply into René's. For every snip the scissors made, she repeated, "Je suis vraiment désolé ('I'm very truly sorry'). Je suis vraiment désolé--"

René's knees struck the cobblestones, as he hurried to collect the locks of hair that fell to the ground; in an attempt to preserve her honor.

"Je suis vraiment désolé," continued Chloé. "Je suis vraiment désolé."

When he finally looked up, he was astonished to discover that she had never been more beautiful. While not able to maintain his position as mayor, from that day forward, they never left each other's side. When asked if he missed his time in politics, René would smile and say, "If I wanted an ulcer, there are more pleasurable ways to get one."

And then, the Second Great War ended; although, life in Brassac had somewhat returned to a semblance of normality after the Germans had fled. On a quiet Wednesday in Autumn, Sister Marie was walking across the Pont-Vieux de Brassac when she saw a scarecrow of a man, crossing towards her. His smile seemed too broad for such a narrow face, and he was fragile; like the russet leaves under the soles of her shoes.

"Marie!" he cried.

She looked at him, puzzled, but could not determine who the

lithe figure might be.

"It's me...it's Francis!" His voice choked, as he struggled to express himself. It had taken the last of his energy to compel her attention.

"Francis!" Marie shouted. "Francis?"

Her heels click-clacked as she sped down the arch of the bridge. She threw herself against him with the balance of emotions she had saved, from a time when she had convinced herself that she could no longer feel. "I'm so sorry. I'm so sorry. Please forgive me Francis."

"Why?" he asked. "Why are you sorry?"

She collapsed, as she sobbed with relief. "I gave up on you. I had completely given you up!"

"I know," he replied. "I know you did! *That* is why I was able to return." Then, his energy restored, he took Marie's arm and led her back to the church; sustaining her, even as she had preserved his memory.

A few months later, Brassac would be the site of an unexpected wedding. Father Jubé officiated while the other sisters served as maids of honor. René walked Noele, who had decided not to become a nun, down the aisle. There he presented her to Léon, to whom she had recently been engaged.

Father Jubé smiled at the bride and wondered if it had all been

Sister Marie's plan, from the beginning. "Relationships are about reconciliation. It is the cornerstone of love, that despite one's transgressions...two sides can be unified in their differences. Let us then not wed the past, but be betrothed to the future."

"Robespierre," yelled Sister Dominique. "Put down that bouquet. Robespierre!"

Though badly scarred, Klaus Metzger survived the series of explosions that killed many of the soldiers that accompanied him; that day at Toulouse-Montaudran airfield. However, when word reached Berlin that a well-respected general had died while in his care, he was imprisoned for the remainder of the war. Because his records were destroyed, when the Soviets arrived, he was able to get a position in the Stassi; where he worked until 1978. His run of luck ended on a clear August morning, when he looked up to see a nun about to cross the street towards him. Having acquired a phobia towards the clergy, he turned to walk in the opposite direction and was immediately struck by a Kübelwagen.

--The End--

ABOUT THE AUTHOR

Fernando Torres, who is also the author of the fantasy novel, <u>The Shadow That Endures</u>, enjoys writing stories that explore the moral dilemmas inherent in the human condition, but from a humorous point-of-view. The son of an American soldier, who participated in the liberation of France, the inspiration for <u>A Habit of Resistance</u> came from his experience as an aviator and time spent listening to friends and family; who were veterans of the Second World War.

For comments or inquiries:

comments@fivetowerspublishing.com

www.fivetowerspublishing.com

ALSO AVAILABLE:

Ian MacDonald lived a solitary, but agreeable existence, in his small Scottish town, until he discovered a mysterious globe that transported him into the multiverse. Little did he realized that, in a world where medieval and rococoesque civilizations struggled for supremacy, he had awakened creatures who sought to right past transgressions; using the ink of men's blood. Some would declare allegiance with dragons while others would sacrifice their lives for honor. For within the darkness if, but a shadow remains...there is light. *The Shadow That Endures* is a humorous, exciting, fantasy-adventure about faith, science, and redemption.

Made in the USA
Lexington, KY
20 March 2015